el puente

Ito Romo

University of New Mexico Press
Albuquerque

First paperbound edition, 2001
ISBN-13: 978-0-8263-2253-1

Library of Congress Cataloging-in-Publication Data
Romo, Ito, 1961–
El puente = The bridge / Ito Romo. —1st paperbound edition.
p. cm.
ISBN 0-8263-2253-0 (alk. paper)
1. Mexican-American women—Fiction 2. Mexican-American Border Region Fiction. 3. Rio Grande—Fiction. 4. Bridges—Fiction. I. Title: Bridge. II. Title.
PS3568.056546 B75 2000
813'.6—dc21 00-008197

Designed by: Linda Mae Tratechaud; LiMiTeD Edition Book Design

To my father,
Refugio Romo, Jr.,
a good man

table of contents

❦

the bridge

1

tomasita

SHE realized her life was out of control when she burned the pot of beans. Now she had to throw them away, a whole kilo. She had to clean the old earthen vessel with a Brillo pad—scouring and scrubbing very hard, until all of the charred blackness was gone—rinsed away—flowing down the Rio Grande, where she emptied her washtub and the sorrow in her soul.

2

carlota

THE five birdcages full of finches hung along the south side of the long room next to the windows facing the Rio Grande. Lorenzo, her mynah bird who ate dry dog food, sat in his cage set on a small, wobbly wooden table by the door. "Meow, meow," the large black bird mimicked. Carlota started yelling, "*¡El gato! El gato!* There's a cat in the house! He's going to eat the birds!" The Chihuahua barked nervously. Sonia, the maid, came running out of the kitchen, across the courtyard—and slipped on the huge pile of watermelon rinds left on the ground for the turtles.

Carlota dropped the box of Kibbles'N Bits that she was about to feed Lorenzo; her two basset hounds, Cowboy and Gina, pushed their way through the screen door and began feeding frantically around her legs, fighting the Chihuahua for the Kibbles, knocking her off balance because of her bad knee. She fell to the ground, but before she went down, she grabbed at Lorenzo's cage in a vain attempt to save herself and accidentally knocked off the wooden clothespin that held the cage door shut. The bird escaped. The dogs chased it. Carlota sat in the middle of the red cement floor of her bedroom, crying, yelling, "*No veo, no veo*," at the top of her lungs, as cataracts began to cover her eyes.

❧

She lived in a twenty-three-room Spanish Colonial house with a courtyard in the middle. Seven of those rooms had been left intact, just as her grandfather had left them one hundred and thirty-six years ago. It was South Texas at the turn of the century: heavy wooden beams holding up eighteen-foot wooden ceilings painted blue, baby blue. There was a powder in the air like an old man's talc that you could see in the light of the evening sun shining through the curtains covering the windows. Three-foot-thick exterior walls painted every three years either yellow, light blue, or pink. And every night she sat in her rocking chair in her living room and stared at the long line of honking cars, trucks, and eighteen-wheelers in front of her house, all of them heading for the bridge two blocks away.

"Oh, how I love to watch the traffic," she'd say. And then sigh.

She sat here the night after Lorenzo had mimicked the cat, after she had fallen, in the dark, and she stared at the traffic, crying, slow tears, her rigid face expressionless, just staring straight ahead as if she could see what she thought had been her miserable life projected in the light beams of the passing autos. Or was it a beautiful life that she could now barely remember? Or was it that cataracts had begun to cover her eyes and no longer let her see the traffic as she used to? Or was it that the cataracts and the tears made the traffic look wet, as if it were raining, and raining always made her want to cry?

Which comes first? she thought. My sadness or my tears?

"*Ya no sé*," she said. She no longer knew.

I don't put a bullet through my head because I have neither the gun nor the courage, she thought as she pushed herself out of the rocking chair and moved her stiff, tired body to her bedroom, where she laid herself down on her grandmother's old bed, the moonlight oozing through the windows, the finches chirping every now and then in their sleep, a strange, cool breeze coming up from the banks of the Rio Grande.

⁂

The following morning, Carlota was making her miniature tortillas. It had been a difficult two days. Her rheumatism was acting up; both legs felt stiff at the knees. Her hip still hurt from the fall, and a deep depression still held her tightly, as tight as the joints in her legs. She looked out the large windows in her kitchen into the backyard. The mulberries had already fallen, and the ground was covered with them, making it easy for the animals to leave their prints all over the hand-laid brick courtyard—little bird prints; strange, almost prehistoric-looking turtle prints; soft-step cat paw prints; and the big, fat prints of the basset hounds. She stared at the hundred-year-old mesquite in the far, south corner, a twenty-foot limb held up by a heavy, thick, rusting chain. She remembered her father building a dirt dam around the tree to make sure it got enough water. She remembered sitting under the tree as a child and chewing on the mesquite pods, sweet and sour. While she stared at the tree, she reached her hand into the tin that held the coffee, and as she was about to throw it into the pot of boiling water, Sonia ran in, screaming.

"*Calo, algo pasa en la televisión,*" Sonia said. Although Sonia could not understand English, she knew the *beep, beep, beep* that announced a coming storm or other possible catastrophe on television. Carlota made her way across the courtyard to see what was happening, slowly, using her cane with each step she took to cross the courtyard into her living room.

"Juan! Juan!" Carlota yelled to her driver and groundskeeper, "Hurry. Go get the car. river is turning red. Hurry! Get the car. Take us to see it!"

It took Juan over an hour to get the car from its parking space around the corner. Carlota was yelling at him when he finally arrived, "What took you so long?"

"I couldn't get through. The traffic is bad. I don't know what's happening," answered the man as he shut the car door after Carlota and Sonia had gotten into the back seat.

"Well, what do you think is happening! Something is going on with the river—that's what's happening. Let's go, let's go!" Carlota spoke to him in a grammatically correct yet highly accented English, keeping her promise to speak to him only in English when he arrived from Mexico five years ago so that he would learn the language.

It took them forty minutes to move one block. Carlota was becoming agitated. And Sonia got nervous because of all the policemen and INS officials in their green outfits standing at almost every corner. As they arrived at Convent, the street that led to the bridge, the policeman directing traffic would not allow them to take a right turn onto the bridge but, rather, made them cross Convent and continue going straight.

"Now what are we going to do?" whined Carlota, her anxiety at a peak.

"Well, I'm going to go straight and follow the street along the river. Maybe we can see something," Juan answered.

The radio announcer had stopped playing country-western music hours ago and was dedicating all the airtime to the news of the day, saying, "The waters of the Rio Grande have turned red. Again, this is a special report—the waters of the Rio Grande have turned red. Downtown traffic is at a standstill. Do not go into the downtown area unless it is an emergency. And if you are planning on going across the river, wait for the next traffic advisory. Right now, eighteen-wheelers are backed up Highway 35 for more than twenty-five miles. Once again, government officials are investigating the strange color of the river. We should have a report from them within the hour."

Juan pointed up to the sky as he stuck his head out of the car window to look at an ABC News helicopter.

"Look, Calo! A helicopter," he said.

At almost every block in the downtown area, there was some kind of broadcasting apparatus, CBS, NBC, ABC, CNN, along with local and area cameramen and reporters.

They followed the street that ran along the top of the high banks of the Rio Grande for almost ten miles. There were so many parked vehicles and so many people perched on the cars and trucks or standing along the edge of the banks that they could not possibly see the river. They couldn't get even a peek. Afraid of falling, Carlota refused to get out, and Sonia ducked, her head low inside the car, so that the INS officials, who weren't even around this far away from the downtown area, would not see her.

Disappointed, Carlota told Juan to return home. She was even more upset after the newscaster reported a sudden thunderstorm on its way to the city. The typically baby blue sky was turning a dark gray, and this made Carlota very nervous; she had an incredible fear of thunder. Once, she had forced a Greyhound bus driver to stop and let her out in the middle of the road on the outskirts of the city because she could see gray clouds ahead from the front seat in the bus. Against all the regulations, the bus driver stopped the bus to let her out because she had begun to scream uncontrollably, almost causing a panic.

It took them over an hour to get back to the house, and even with all of that, Juan had to drop them off half a block from the door. Just as Carlota entered the door, Sonia still hiding in the car from the "*migra*," the sky let loose with a shattering boom. Carlota yelled. The thunderstorm erupted.

A couple of hours later, after the storm ended and the city was engulfed in bright South Texas sunlight and unbearable humidity, Carlota asked Juan to get the car again.

"*Ándale*, Juan," she said, "go get the car. Let's see if we can see the river."

Juan left once again to try to maneuver the car back to the front of the house. It was almost impossible with this kind of traffic, but he succeeded. Within twenty minutes, he was in front of the house, helping Carlota into the backseat.

Sonia refused to come because, she said, "There are too many policemen and immigration people out there."

Just as Juan got back in the car and closed the door, an eighteen-wheeler stopped for a fraction of a second and gave him enough time to get into the lane that led toward the bridge.

For forty-five minutes, Juan was stepping on the gas, guiding the car about three feet forward, and stepping on the brakes again. He had to turn the air conditioner off and keep the windows rolled down so that the car would not overheat. Perspiration rolled off his forehead. He kept wiping it away, talking incessantly while Carlota watched all the commotion outside the car window. She did not perspire; she never did.

They finally got to the bridge, paid the toll, and slowly rolled on. It took Juan over an hour to travel one quarter of the length of the bridge. Now, Carlota's nerves were beginning to come undone again. She couldn't see the river's water from the car, there were so many people, cameras, and policemen all along the bridge. Her anxiety was mounting. Knowing that she was about to start yelling at him to turn around right there and then—which would have been impossible—Juan suggested that she get out of the car and look over the handrail.

She said, "Yes."

He was completely astounded. Never had he expected her to agree. He thought she wouldn't even think of it, and they would get into an argument, and with this argument, he could distract her from erupting—although he was very used to dealing with it. This way, she wouldn't insist that he turn around or stop the car and walk her home—or something just as absurd.

He put the car in park, and since traffic was moving so slowly, he got out of the car, went around to the back, opened Carlota's door, and helped her onto the sidewalk. Then he ran back to the car and got in; the cars in line behind him were beginning to honk. He heard Carlota yelling for him not to go too far.

He asked himself under his breath, "Where the hell am I supposed to go?"

Doing something no one would ever have expected her to do, Carlota cautiously pushed her way through the crowd, holding tightly to her cane, telling those in her way, "Please let me through. I want to see the river. I'm an old lady, look. I can't even walk. Please let me see."

She finally squeezed her way to the rail and looked out over the side of the bridge. When she saw the river, she could not believe it. The water was dark, dark red, as far as the eye could see. A woman pushed her aside to get a view of the river, and this made her lose her balance. She yelled, and a young man standing next to her tried to hold her up, but as he grabbed her arm to keep her from falling, an eighteen-wheeler blew its horn and loudly screeched to a halt in front of two old men running across the street, startling the young man, making him lose his grip on Carlota. She almost fell to the sidewalk, everything spinning around her, the wind from a low-flying helicopter above, the smell of mulberries, mulberries everywhere. But the young man regained his grip on her arm and saved her.

"What happened, young man?" she asked.

The young man pointed across the bridge and said, "Those two men almost got run over by a truck."

She remembered Juan and the car and started looking around for him frantically. She spotted him about fifteen feet away. She asked the young man to please help her back to the car, and as she grabbed his arm to help herself walk, she looked across the bridge and saw a young woman squatting, two old men giving her their shirts so that she could rest her head against the rail of the bridge, and an older woman kneeling in front of her, holding a newborn baby. The sidewalk was covered with blood. People were yelling frantically for an ambulance. The old woman held the child tenderly, wiping the baby's face with the hem of her ancient housedress.

Looking straight ahead at the long line of cars in front of her, Carlota cried quietly, "Juan. Juan."

SHE had her work skirt taken in so much that the back pockets met right at the crack. Ten years of waitressing at the Southland Cafe had put on fifty pounds. Then, slowly, she had lost them. But she would only have the skirts taken in—not cut—just in case she gained the weight back. She had also lost one of her front teeth, the left one—from eating all those sugar doughnuts all those years.

She had bitten into a candy apple, and the tooth had snapped right off, falling into a vent blowing hot air out of the sidewalk downtown. She had started speaking to her customers out of the side of her mouth as if she had had a stroke and half her face had been paralyzed. She could not stop touching the little stump with the tip of her tongue.

"I'm goin' across the river in the morning to get this fixed," she finally said one day to all of her customers, smiling, a big black hole right up front, the little stump barely showing, almost as if she was proud of her missing tooth, "'cause it's a lot cheaper."

"She, the dentist, she's gonna make me a bridge," she continued. "She can make it overnight. It'll be ready tomorrow. She's goooooood, really goooooood and faaaaaast! Goooooood faaaaaast, faaaaaast goooooood!"

The next day, as she was about to leave work after her early afternoon shift and walk across the bridge to get her tooth, she turned on the TV set that sat on the cigarette machine by the entrance to the kitchen and saw CNN Special Report flashing across the screen.

She recognized the bridge, the river, and started yelling frantically, "Oh, my God! It's the bridge. Look, everybody, the bridge, the bridge—it's on TV."

Everyone stared with mouths open in disbelief as they saw the very same river that was only a few blocks away, red as the filling in the cherry pie in the mirrored, overhead icebox.

"I'm supposed to go get my tooth made right now. Now they're not gonna let me cross," she whined after all the commotion subsided. "What do I do?" she asked the manager, and without waiting for a response, she added, "I'm gonna go see. I'll come back later to tell you what happened. Oh, my God, and it's gonna rain!"

Not two blocks away from the Southland Cafe, the sky let loose with an explosive boom. An artificial little scream popped out of Cindy's mouth. (She had never really yelled out loud before in her life. Her mother had told her that if you yelled or screamed, your cheekbones would grow too much, and you wouldn't look like a lady, you'd look like a horse. So she never yelled or screamed, only tiny, little fake screams.) She ran to the entrance of Vogue Fashions down the street and stayed there until the last raindrop fell. She could not risk her hairdo.

"It'll fall all apart if it gets wet," she thought out loud.

She had gone to the hairdresser the day before yesterday and had slept very carefully, on her back, not moving a bit—as if she were dead—for three consecutive days, until her next appointment. The entrance to Vogue Fashions on Houston Street was big and beautifully tiled with images of the sun. She spent at least ten minutes there every day putting on her makeup before she went to work, staring at her reflection in the glass of the huge windows. Today, though, she was more interested in getting across the river to the dentist. She just didn't have it in her to make sure she looked "really good." The rain, the idea of sitting in the dentist chair for hours, knowing that she would slobber and come back feeling as if her lip weighed seventy-five pounds, made her forget how she always had to "look good, really good." And, of course, she was curious as to what was going on at the bridge—so she hurried.

As she got closer to the bridge, she began to realize, "This is a big deal, a really *big* deal." And as she turned the corner onto Convent, she saw the first TV camera and transformed herself. Instead of going south when she reached Convent, she turned right toward the JC Penney. She needed to freshen up her makeup, and, "Those windows are perfect. Not as good as Vogue, mind you, but still perfect for doing makeup." She stood there in front of the big window and rubbed the makeup-encrusted compact pad into the bright pink powder and then onto her face.

What if they ask me somethееng? she thought.

With one last push of a hairpin back into her pouf, she began to strut toward the bridge. Her breasts were suddenly higher and fuller, her back was perfectly straight, and she walked the same way they had taught her to walk at the model workshop she had taken at the Plaza Hotel with all those famous models from San Antonio.

"They were in the Sears catalog," she had said to her friends at the Southland Cafe. "That's the only reason I'm gonna go."

But by the time she arrived at the bridge, there were two lines for pedestrians, both backed up for three whole blocks, so many people had come to see. She squinted, holding her hands over her eyes to shield them from the sun, to see which line led to the TV reporter she had noticed standing at the entrance to the bridge. Although she always said, "*Estoy bien ciega*," she had spotted the camera almost immediately. She figured out which line it was and made her way to the end of it.

It took her half an hour to get onto the bridge.

"They were only letting a few people at a time get on the bridge," she reported at the Southland the following morning. "It took me forever to cross!"

Right before she stepped up to the turnstile, before reaching the reporter and the cameraman, she pinched her cheeks hard to make more color rise in them. She forced a big smile onto her face—thinking about the modeling class again—when she suddenly remembered the tooth and cut her smile down to half the size, daintily placing her hand over her mouth.

She acted totally surprised when the reporter from the CBS affiliate in Dallas put a microphone up to her face. Smiling softly, she placed her hand over her mouth again.

"Miss, have you seen the river?" asked the reporter.

"Oh, yes," she answered—although she hadn't. "It's everywhere on the TB stations," she continued. "Some people are saying it's a miracle. You know, that the water gives you miracles. I even heard on Mexican TB that the Pope is sending those special priests that check for the miracles"—although she hadn't seen the reports on Mexican TV, either.

The reporter said, "Thank you, miss," and sort of pushed her through onto the bridge, more interested in what an old lady carrying a tinfoil-covered dish had to say.

As she walked on the bridge, she felt famous. Helicopters with cameras above her, more cameras and reporters everywhere, people staring at her after she had spoken to the reporter—or so she thought—all this made her eyes glaze over.

She began to plan "to become famous!"

Cindy turned around, although she was already halfway across the bridge and, for the first time ever, yelled at the top of her lungs. "When I'm coming out on the TB?"

She was waving her hands wildly above her head to try to catch the reporter's attention, completely oblivious to the huge, gaping hole in her mouth—lost in her newfound fame.

She kept waving her hands, trying to get the reporter's attention, until a loud honk scared her almost as much as the thunder had earlier, and she yelled again, a false, little scream this time. She recovered her composure, remembering the hole in her mouth, and she placed her hand over it again, all ladylike.

She took a big, deep breath of the strange, mulberried air, straightened her shoulders, stared at the red water for just seconds out of the corner of her eyes, and swayed her hips across the rest of the bridge.

"Hollygwood, here comes Cindy!"

When she arrived that afternoon at the dentist's humble office close to the red-light district, she wondered if she had made the right choice. She paid the cabdriver and asked him several times if he was sure he had taken her to the right address: no sign, an old wooden door, a dog playing with a dead bird, just a simple 753 Pereida painted above the entrance in red paint that had dripped. She thought of blood and put her hand up to her mouth as the taxi sped away.

She opened the door into a little room with three wooden chairs and a newspaper thrown on the floor in the corner, a big, full-color, half-page picture of the bridge. The picture on the front page of the red water running under the bridge reminded her of blood again and made her begin to think that the color red and the blood itself were omens. A wicked smile came to her lips when she remembered the TV reporter, and she imagined herself on the TV set at the Southland. She took a few steps forward and knocked on the door in the middle of the room.

"¿Sí?" someone asked from behind the door.

Cindy peeked her head through the door and answered, *"¿La Doctora?"* thinking that she was talking to the doctor's assistant.

But the recent graduate didn't have the money to pay for an assistant yet; she answered, "I'm the doctor, Señorita Rodriguez. Come on in."

The back room where the dentist worked was even smaller than the front room, but because it was in the back, it had to do. The dentist asked Cindy to sit down on the chair, and after looking for a short while, she explained the procedure to Cindy: a root canal on the little stump that was left, an impression to make sure the new tooth fit, and, then, a superbonding agent to keep the tooth in place "forever."

"I will do it all—no need to send it out; it'll just take longer," she said to Cindy, but really, she just couldn't afford to send anything out, and at the end of her explanation, "The tooth will be ready by tomorrow after one o'clock."

"You're not even gonna take an x ray?" Cindy asked the doctor in Spanish.

"No. You're going to need a root canal anyway to strengthen the false tooth. I would usually take an x ray to see if there is any decay, but since we're doing the root canal, you don't really need one," the dentist explained, continuing in Spanish.

Although she had managed to buy the x-ray equipment, she still couldn't buy any film.

Cindy felt like leaping out of the chair and running all the way back across the bridge, but she knew that this situation was perfect for her plan. Since the doctor did all the work herself, all Cindy had to do was destroy the impression, the mold. Since the doctor was not taking any x rays, there would be no medical evidence; since Cindy was paying in cash, there would be no record of the transaction—it would be her word against the dentist's. Who were they going to believe, a hardworking American girl like herself or some two-bit Mexican dentist who couldn't even afford to have a decent office on Guerrero like all the other dentists that serviced the Americans?

"Go ahead, Doctor," she said.

⁂

Late that afternoon, Cindy had to cover the graveyard shift for one of the new young waitresses who was going to her high school prom. Her entire mouth was asleep, and it felt as if she had been stung by a thousand killer bees. But actually, she didn't feel a thing; her head was spinning. She was so far into the plan, she was dizzy. She could not turn back.

At the Southland, she lied. She told everyone that she had not been able to cross the bridge, that she had waited in line for over an hour and when she finally got onto the bridge, there were so many people that she hadn't been able to get over to the Mexican side. She tried to push her way through the crowd but couldn't even move.

"We were like the sardines in those cans," she said, pointing to the cans of tuna on the shelf behind the counter.

"I gave up," she told them, "and went home for a few hours because my tooth hurt too much. I only came in so that that poor little girl can go to her high school prom—I never got to go to mine, you know."

She ran around the Southland, taking orders absentmindedly, sometimes right, sometimes wrong. Instead of ham and eggs, she would order *chorizo con huevo*; instead of flour tortillas, she served her customers white toast. Although she couldn't really remember much about that afternoon, the novocaine having numbed her brain as well as her mouth, all she could think of was the evening news. The one thing she did remember was the NBC on the reporter's microphone. When she walked into the Southland that afternoon around four o'clock, she had immediately run to the television and flipped to channel six. (The old TV had no remote.) When anyone even came close to the TV set, whether it was a customer or another waitress, she would grunt and growl from across the huge dining room since her dental work did not allow her to talk much without feeling an incredible amount of pain. Everyone understood they could not change the channel. She didn't tell anybody that she might be on TV because she had to act surprised; it was part of her plan, part of her "internachonal TB debut."

When the evening news began, Cindy literally stopped in her tracks and the customers stopped eating; they knew that the bridge would be the first thing that would come on. She took off her apron—signifying that she was off—and placed it on the counter next to the Boston cream pie.

"Good evening, I'm Tom Brokaw. The story of what seems to be a potential environmental disaster of catastrophic proportions is still unraveling in South Texas as a joint team of scientists from the Centers for Disease Control and the Environmental Protection Agency continued its investigation in a typically quiet community on the border between the U.S. and Mexico. Here's Albert Torres with a report from the Rio Grande."

Cindy let out a sharp cry from behind her hand when Torres popped onto the television screen. She was disappointed when she saw that the one who was now on TV was not the one who had interviewed her, but she knew that it would not be the only report on the river that evening. In anticipation, she chewed on the skin of her palm with the little stump in the front of her mouth. The reporter was talking about the possibility of industrial waste being the cause of the color of the river. He interviewed a member of the joint team investigating the incident who said that the results of tests being performed on the water samples taken from the river early that morning would not be ready until tomorrow morning and that in the meantime, any information that he could provide would be strictly speculation.

"So, as you can see, Tom, we'll have to wait until tomorrow for any real information about the river," said the reporter.

"Thank you, Albert," said Tom Brokaw. He continued, "Although this city in South Texas is used to a great deal of international trade and interaction and is, in fact, the largest inland port in the United States, it hasn't received this kind of international media attention since President Richard Nixon visited during his reelection campaign in 1972. Here's our local NBC correspondent, Mike Aguilar, with a report on how all this commotion is affecting the citizens along the border . . . Mike."

"Well, Tom, I talked to a lot of people here last night during the evening rush hour, when thousands upon thousands cross the bridge back to their homes on the Mexican side, and again earlier today during the lunchtime rush hour, to find out what they thought not only about the color of the river but also about all this media coverage that has virtually taken over the bustling downtown area overnight," said the reporter.

"Oh, my God, it's him!" Cindy realized.

After interviewing several people at the same place where she had been interviewed, Cindy whimpered when she saw the image of the old woman who had been interviewed after her pop onto the screen. She squinted and saw herself walking off behind the reporter. She wanted to cry.

She almost ran up to the TV and pointed out to everyone at the Southland, "That woman with her back to the camera, the one with the green dress, yes, that one, that's me!"

But she knew she couldn't. It might give her away. It might make everyone think that she wanted to be on TV, that she wanted to be a star. She would wait until tomorrow. Everyone would see her. As the reporter was winding up, saying that he would be back tomorrow morning with any breaking news, Cindy saw herself again, tiny, way down the bridge, wildly waving her hands in the air. She turned around quietly, tied her apron back on, and went to the back of the kitchen, where she stepped into the small dishwashing room and lit a cigarette, sucking the smoke in through the tooth hole in her mouth, hating the reporter for "cutting me out."

Just you wait, Mike Aguilar! Tomorrow I'll go to another reporter with a story that'll make him famous. Just you wait. You'll be sorry! she thought, and flicked her ashes into the shiny stainless-steel drain in the middle of the floor.

The next morning, around eleven o'clock, Cindy took the bus from her home downtown; she had asked her manager for the evening shift so she would have a chance to "try again to go across the river."

She took the bus this time from the bridge to the dentist's office to make sure that no one would be able to identify her. (She had to take every precaution.) She even got off of the bus several blocks from the dentist's office to make sure that no one on the bus would make a connection.

Looking around, she walked rapidly toward the door of the office and sidled in, looking over her shoulder again as if she were in a thriller. She went straight to the back door, and without knocking or announcing herself, she stepped right in. The doctor was putting the finishing touches on her new tooth, which was temporarily fixed to a negative mold of her upper jaw.

She thought anxiously, There must be two molds.

She surveyed the dentist's working area and, within seconds, discovered a second impression. Now she had to destroy two instead of one like she had planned.

How am I gonna do it? How am I gonna do it? she was asking herself over and over again.

At the instruction of the dentist, she lay down on the reclining chair. It took the dentist a few minutes to mix the solution to bond Cindy's tooth to the little stump in the front of her mouth. In about twenty minutes, the whole procedure was over, and Cindy had a brand-new tooth.

She ran her tongue over the front of her teeth to see how it felt and said, "It feels goooood! And faaaaast!"

The dentist asked her if she wanted to have her teeth cleaned, and Cindy asked her, "How much?"

The dentist mentioned a small fee, and although it was nothing compared to American standards, Cindy had not even thought about having her teeth cleaned and had not brought any more money than what she needed to pay the dentist for the root canal and the new tooth, the bus, the bridge, and the corn on the cob she had planned to buy on her way back home to celebrate.

Finally I can eat a corn on the cob again, she thought.

When the dentist left her side to wash her hands in the little sink adjacent to the x-ray machine, Cindy let out a yell and acted as if she was falling out of the chair. Cindy grabbed hold of the small worktable to gain her balance and yanked the oilcloth from the table, throwing everything on it to the floor. Cindy surveyed the damage immediately—both impressions had been shattered.

What a performance! she thought, and then apologized profusely for the mess and began immediately to try to put all the dentist's instruments back on the table.

The dentist told her not to worry. Cindy faked tears. The dentist assured her that nothing had happened to anything except to her impressions, which were not good anymore anyway. The only other broken thing was a small, round mirror that the dentist was about to have her look into to see her teeth.

The dentist pulled a couple of tissues from a box of Kleenex by the sink and tried to comfort Cindy, who was now crying uncontrollably.

"Don't worry," she said again. "I'm only sorry that you won't be able to see how beautiful your new tooth looks because that was the only mirror I had."

Red, blood, and now a broken mirror, thought Cindy. Oh, my God!

Cindy let out another loud cry. The dentist poured a cup of purified water for Cindy from a plastic jug. (She did not feel that it was safe to use the water from the faucet since infection might set in.) After a few small gulps, Cindy regained her composure, stood up and fixed her skirt, and paid the doctor, apologizing incessantly. She quickly got "the hell out of Dodge"—she had heard that in a Western she had seen last night on TBS right before she fell asleep.

She headed to the bridge, erasing every little bit of that dentist and that office and that area of the city from her mind. She walked determinedly for about a mile, again looking behind her every few steps to make sure that no one was following her. At the corner of Pino

Suarez and Nacataz, she boarded a green bus headed toward the bridge.

She sat where she thought she was "inconspic, inconspicously, inconspiculous, whatever," at the back, next to an old lady holding a cage with two chickens in it. She pulled out her compact and quickly slapped on her pink blush.

She ran her tongue over her teeth again to make sure the new tooth felt right and thought, Gooood and faaaast! Goooood and faaaaast!

⁂

The bus dropped her off half a block from the bridge. As she stepped off of the bus, she made the sign of the cross, yanked down her skirt, fiddled with a bobby pin that stuck out a bit, pulled her shoulders back, and thought one more time, Hollygwood, here comes Cindy!

As soon as she set foot on the bridge, she began looking for the reporters. There were so many of them that she didn't know which one to choose, who was the most famous. Directly in front of her, about twenty feet away, she saw a woman holding a camera with a big, red sticker that read CNN. A young, well-dressed, blond *americana* was standing in front of the camerawoman, speaking into a microphone, obviously broadcasting. Cindy needed to act quickly. Without thinking about it any longer, she strutted toward the woman, and when she reached her, she fell on her knees, sobbing.

"It's a miracle! It's a miracle! Look! Look!" Cindy cried, pointing at her new tooth. "My tooth, it growed back! I broke it two months ago, and I was going to the dentist, and look, look, it growed back! Oh, my God! Oh, my God! It's a miracle! A little boy over there. Where is he? Over there, oh, my God, he's gone. He gave me some water from the river, and when I drunk it, I felt like fainting, and then I had a lot of pain in my mouf, and then—then the tooth was there! Oh, my God! Oh, my God! It's a miracle! Dear Jesus, a miracle."

The camera was rolling. Cindy's tears turned pink as they fell down over her cheeks onto the hot, South Texas pavement.

4

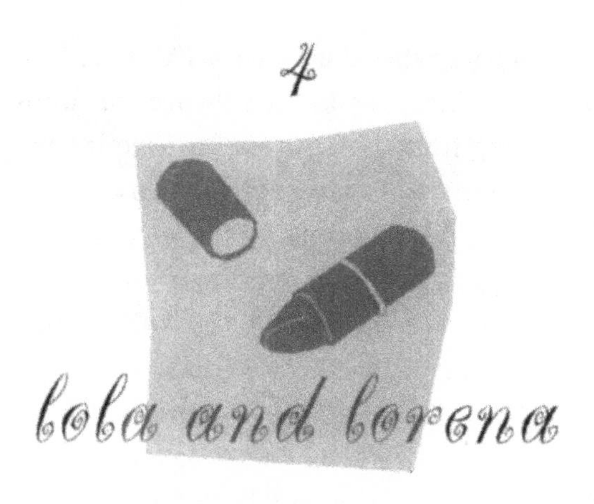

lola and lorena

THE two girls in blue jean miniskirts and tight, stretch tube tops were sharing a lipstick at the bus stop when the lipstick slipped from their hands as they passed it to each other and fell right into a crack in the cement sidewalk and got jammed so hard neither of them could pry it out when they squatted down to try because they didn't want to break off their Lee press-on nails.

"Whatsamatter with you, Lorena?" one of them said to the other. "I just bought that lipstick at Walgreens. It costed me seven dollars. You better pay me back, bitch!"

"*Ay*, Lola," Lorena answered. "It wasn't my fault. I'm all sweaty. It's hot! The lipstick fell right out of my hand like a Butterfingers."

"What?" asked Lola. "What do you mean like a Butterfingers?"

"That's what they say on TV when someone hits something and it falls over or drops something from their hands, just like it happened to me right now," said Lorena. "You should say, '*Mira*, Lorena, you're such a butterfingers,'" and Lorena laughed.

"Lorena, I don't think you know what you're talking about, girl," said Lola.

"Shut up," answered Lorena.

"No, you shut up. Just wait for the bus and shut up. I don't want to talk to you no more," said one girl to the other.

You could see the heat coming out of the doors of the bakery where they waited for the bus to go downtown. It had peeled the paint off the homemade wooden sign above the doors, Sonia's Bakery.

Above the peeling sign, yards of exposed wires held together with old electrical tape that did not stick anymore dangled, connecting the tiny radio inside the bakery to an old, gray, megaphone-shaped speaker crudely screwed onto the side of the wall next to where the girls were standing.

"Oh, it's my song," yelled Lola, stumbling frantically through the doors of Sonia's Bakery in her one-size-too-small, high-heeled shoes.

A few seconds later, she pulled a fat, middle-aged woman out of the bakery by the hand. The woman was holding on to the hand of

another woman who was holding the hand of
another woman who was holding the hand of
another woman who was holding the hand of
another woman, all sweating profusely in their
white, flour-covered aprons tied tight at the
waist, their hair pushed into thick black nets,
streaming out of the bakery like the monkeys
from a Barrel of Monkeys.

"Okay, everybody, get in line. Hurry up! The song's gonna finish," whined Lola as if she were a famous choreographer.

"Now, step, ball, change. Step, ball, change. No, Mary, not like that—like this," she said to the first woman she had pulled out from the bakery.

Lola tried to turn gracefully, holding her hands up and to the side, both pinkies out, but her foot bent right at the heel, and she yelled, *"¡Ayyyy!"* But she gathered her composure like the true professional she thought she was and continued, "Step back, step back. Now, turn. Good! Good! You all look beautiful. You all look wonderful. You all look fabulous. Oh, I love this song."

The music, full of static, blared. They danced happily, sweating, tripping, stumbling, but dancing, under the hot South Texas sun, until they saw the bus coming up the street.

"C'mon, Lola!" yelled Lorena. "The bus is coming."

Lorena looked down the avenue and saw the city bus about a block away.

"One, two, three, four, spin. Oh, my God, we have to go, girls," she said to the women as she started running to the corner to catch the bus. "I love you. I really love you. You're beautiful! You're fabulous."

The women from the bakery waved at them as they ran toward the bus, Lola again tripping because of her high heels and cursing in Spanish, *"¡Pinches zapatos pendejos!"*

They sat together in the only seats left on the bus.

Lola said, "*Ay*, Lorena, don't get so close to me. You're all hot and sweaty! *¡Uy!* Look, your sweat is all over my dress. You're gonna have to buy me a new one. Look, I bet you it's stained. *Ay*, Lorena, you're so . . . so . . . so sticky. Yes, you're sticky. Did you put on deodorant? 'Cause it smells funny. I think you stink, Lorena. Lorena, you're sticky and stinky, ha, ha, ha!"

"Shut up, Lola. You're a *puta*," Lorena said to her, and continued, "You're *basura*! Trash. That's what you are. You're *basura* trash. That's all I know," and she got up and squeezed into a seat next to an old man, who turned around and said, "*Buenas tardes, señorita*."

She said to Lola, "See, Lola. I'm a *señorita*, not a used *basura* trash bag like you."

Lola pulled a file out of her little purse with a long strap and began to file her nails and said, "I'm ignoring you, Lorena. Look at me, I'm ignoring you. Shut up and don't talk to me anymore until we get downtown. No. No. Don't talk to me anymore until we get downtown."

She looked out the window toward the east to the other side of Highway 35 and murmured, "Oh, my God, it's gonna rain!"

Just as they arrived at St. Thomas Plaza, where they were supposed to get off, the clouds exploded and almost everyone in the bus yelled. Lola grabbed a newspaper that had been left on the floor of the bus, put it over her head, and ran toward the awning of the Rexall Drugs on the corner. Lorena followed her to the sidewalk, and they both went inside.

The old woman, black glasses hanging from a silver chain around her neck, said hello to her familiar customers and asked them how they were.

"Oh, I was fine," said Lola, "until this rain came. Now my hair is falling!"

She stared into the mirror at the cosmetics counter, trying to push her hair back into place.

"Miss Perez," said Lorena, "do you have a lip-stick called Raspberry Cream? Lola lent me one she bought at the Walgreens, and it got stuck in the sidewalk when we were dancing. Now she wants me to buy her one like it. Do you have one?"

"No, honey," answered Miss Perez, a bit puzzled about the dancing but knowing better than to ask any questions, "not Raspberry Cream, but I do have one called Raspberry Freeze, and it has the spearmint in it and feels cool, real cold when you put it on the lips. Here, come here, come try it."

Lorena made her way over to the counter behind which Miss Perez was standing, but Lola jumped off the tall chair she had immediately taken when she arrived and pushed Lorena out of the way, saying, "No, Lorena. The lipstick is for me, Miss Perez. Show it to me. Let me try it."

Lola tried the lipstick on her lips and gave it back to Miss Perez, who wiped it with a cotton ball and then handed it to Lorena to try on too.

"Oh, Lola," said Miss Perez, "it looks beautiful on you. Look!"

She handed her a small, round mirror and said, "It looks beautiful. So, so red. Just like the river."

Lola gave Miss Perez a questioning look and asked, "What do you mean, 'like the river'?"

Miss Perez asked, "Oh, my God, don't you know? The river is red. Something happened. Haven't you seen the TV? The river, it's all red. Nobody knows what's a matter with it, but it's all red, red, red . . . dark red, like the lipstick!"

"No!" answered Lorena. "What happened? How come it's red?"

"Nobody knows," said Miss Perez. "There are investigators here from Washington or somewhere trying to find out why, but nobody knows. But everybody is over there. All the TV stations from all over the world. They say that even that man, Tom Prokob, from CBS got here this morning. I don't know, mind you, I haven't seen him, but Miss Jones from Richer's Department Store told me that he had came in to buy a tie. Imagine, he forgot all of his ties back in Washington or New York or wherever he lives."

"Oh, my God, Lorena, let's go!" said Lola. "I want to see what's happening."

"Lola," answered Lorena, pointing out the window, "look outside, please! It's raining cats and dogs. Mira! You want to get wet?"

"Shut up," Lola answered. "Pay for the lipstick. You owe me. Miss Perez, she's paying for this lipstick. Ooh! It feels so cool." And she continued as she licked her lips, "I like it, Miss Perez. It's nice red. I don't need a bag."

She slipped the lipstick into her little purse with its long strap.

The rain stopped just about as quickly as it had started. It only took one Coke at the fountain, and they shared it.

"Come on, Lorena," Lola said, pointing at a speeding van. "Look, there goes CBS. Hurry!"

"Golly," whined Lorena. "It's so hot."

When Lola pulled open the glass door, a gust of brutal, humid air hit them. They hurried toward the bridge, Lola tripping again in her high heels.

They were both amazed, dumbfounded really, when they turned the corner from Hidalgo onto Convent. As far as they could see when they looked toward the bridge, there were hundreds, maybe thousands of people. The streets were gridlocked with cars, trucks, emergency vehicles, and eighteen-wheelers.

Lola said to Lorena, "Close your mouf, girl. It's very unladylike to let your tongue hang out like that. A bug's gonna fly in."

"Oh, my God," Lorena said. "I've never seen so many people here. Not even when they used to let everyone in from the other side without papers. What was that called?"

"Lorena," answered Lola, "you're crazy. They never let everyone in without papers."

"No, Lola, my mother told me that they used to open the bridge once a year during the festival and let anyone who wanted to come across come over," said Lorena.

"Well, then, your mother is crazy too," answered Lola.

"Don't say bad things about my mother, Lola. You're a bitch. May she rest in peace," said Lorena, and made the sign of the cross.

They continued to walk toward the bridge. Two blocks away from it, a fat taxi driver whistled at Lola, then yelled, "Hey, *mamacita*, you have nice, big legs just like my fat wife. C'mon over here so I can show you what a real man is like."

"Fuck you," yelled Lola, and shot the finger at the fat taxi driver, who was hanging out with three others by a phone on a telephone pole where they received their calls.

"No, you big *joto*," answered the taxi driver, "you're the one who likes to get fucked and up the butt."

Lola ran to the taxi driver and began hitting him with her purse. The taxi driver punched her right in the face, and Lola fell to the hot, wet pavement. Lorena ran up to the fat taxi driver and kicked him hard in the groin.

That's when the cops arrived. They pushed Lola back to the ground as she tried to get up, and one of the cops put her in a choke hold. Lorena began yelling, "*Pinche policía pendejo*" at the cops, so they let go of Lola and started walking toward her.

"Run, Lola," Lorena yelled. "Run across the bridge. They can't get you there!"

Lola got up, still dizzy, and began to run toward the entrance to the bridge. She tripped again because of her high heels, so she bent over, took them off, grabbed them in one hand, and threw an empty soda can at the fat taxi driver, who was sitting on the sidewalk comforting his genitals. She ran as fast as she could toward the turnstiles at the entrance to the bridge, a desperado riding her horse across the river.

By this time, the cops were laughing at what had happened, and they let Lorena go. She walked away quickly, trying to catch up with Lola, already halfway down the bridge, still running.

"Wait, Lola," yelled Lorena. "Wait for me!"

Lola turned around when she heard Lorena and almost fell because an eighteen-wheeler honked right next to her. She bent over to put her heels back on, and as she did, she looked ahead of her and saw a woman giving birth, a helicopter flying steadily above her with a cameraman hanging out the door, catching it all on film.

"Lola," yelled Lorena, catching up with her.

She grabbed Lola by the shoulder and made her lose the balance she had just regained in her high heels. Lola tripped, and when she did, she leapt forward, falling flat on her face, her nose against the pavement. The strange mixture of the smell of hot tar from the street and mulberries from the river's water filled her nostrils. Her purse popped open when it hit the pavement in front of her, the brand-new lipstick popped out too, and all she could do was watch it roll slowly across the sidewalk to the edge of the bridge and drop into the red, red Rio Grande.

5

ESTELA left her husband of fifty-seven years at the age of seventy-five. She packed a couple of housedresses into her plastic mesh bag and walked to the American side of the river, following the same route she took every day—only this time it was for good.

She would never come back to this damned Mexico and her damned Mexican husband. She went straight to the candy counter at the JC Penney on Convent and bought herself a pound of chocolate-covered raisins, hoping they would not melt from the heat of the hot South Texas sun before she ate them. The smell of chocolate, popcorn, and cheap polyester blowing from the vents cooled her as she walked into the store that morning. After she bought her Raisinets, she stood there, staring at the escalators, popping the candy into her mouth, one by one, dazed, resting from the heat, light perspiration on her upper lip.

She suddenly remembered the huge fight she had had with her husband right outside the store, years and years ago, just half a block away, right there on the corner of Convent and Lincoln, the day the president had come to town. She remembered the famous picture of Richard Nixon standing up in a convertible, hands raised in victory, Woolworth in between them, the intense morning heat radiating, pearlescent, off the black motorcade. She stood there that hot day in May, angry, frustrated, confused, eating chocolate-covered raisins, her face as red as the day was hot, wondering if the president of the United States ever fought with his wife.

The fighting had gone on for years.

*

"*¿Qué calor, verdad?*" someone said to her, lightly patting her on her back.

When she looked over her shoulder, no one was there.

This heat is making me crazy, she thought, and walked out the doors and down the street on Convent. Looking toward the bridge, Convent ran right onto the bridge, and the bridge ran right onto Guerrero. Guerrero became Convent. Convent became Guerrero. Two different streets. Two different countries. Two different worlds. Hot black pavement separating them. That's all.

She touched her hand to her breast, making sure the small package she had smuggled across the bridge that morning was still there in her bra.

⁂

"Oh, Lucita," said Estela to her niece in Spanish. "Thank you so much for letting me stay here, *hija*."

"*Tía*, you know that you can stay here whenever you want. My little apartment is your apartment," said Lucita as she grabbed her luggage. She was on her way to San Antonio for the long weekend with some girlfriends from work. She continued, "Make sure you lock the door at night, *Tía*. I'll be back Sunday night. There's lots of food in the refrigerator. I left the phone number of the hotel on the refrigerator. Call me if you need anything. I love you."

"Bye, *hija*," said Estela. "Thank you. *Vaya con Dios*."

As soon as the car was out of sight, Estela grabbed her purse and headed to the supermarket several blocks away. It was only ten o'clock in the morning, yet the heat from the day before could still be felt oozing up from the ground.

I'm going to get there and set the table for his dinner the same way I did for so many godforsaken days, she thought in Spanish. Thank God I kept the key to the house. He's going to pay for every one of those maids he slept with. He's going to pay for never giving me a single penny the whole fifty-something years we were together. How long were we together? I don't even remember. Oh, Roberto, you're going to pay. *Lo voy a matar.*

The supermarket was incredibly crowded and incredibly cold. She knew this and had brought her shawl with her. The glass doors opened automatically as she walked up to them, and she quickly grabbed a cart to help her hold herself up as she walked. As able-bodied as she knew she still was, the last few days had drained her, and the heat, the heat was just too much to bear. She went straight to the Mexican food section first. She looked for the glass jars of mole paste for a long time before she finally spotted them on the opposite side of the aisle. She also needed bread, Mexican chocolate that came in a block, peanut butter, garlic, pepper, a Pyrex dish, a small roll of tinfoil, and, of course, chicken, breasts only—that's all he would eat.

"The rest," he would say, "the dark meat, is for the poor." He really meant that the dark meat was for her.

She bought everything she needed because she didn't want to use anything from her niece's cupboard. She did not want to involve her in what she was going to do. As she made her way to the checkout stands, she raised her hand to her bosom again, making sure the little pouch was still there. When she felt it, her heart began to race. She felt faint but wide awake.

She made her way back slowly to her niece's house. When she arrived, bathed in perspiration, she immediately, almost before closing and locking the door behind her, began to undress to take a shower. When she took her housedress off over her head, the little pouch she had been carrying popped out of her bra and fell on the floor. She looked at it; she stared and stared and stared for what she thought was a long time.

The package of chicken was no longer cold. Naked, she picked the package of chicken breasts up from off the floor and went to the kitchen to put it in the refrigerator. She poked a little hole in the plastic to make sure the chicken had not spoiled.

He won't even think of touching it if he thinks it's spoiled, she thought, feeling just a slight bit of moisture on the tip of her nose where it had touched the package.

She went to the bathroom, carefully, as if her old bones had, within the past few days, become heavy yet brittle. Once in the bathroom, she had a difficult time adjusting the newfangled knobs that controlled the temperature of the water, so much time it seemed, that she had the time to think. She decided to take a bath instead. She threw several of the clear, pink bubble-bath beads that her niece had on the bathroom countertop next to the sink into the water, then she realized she had not placed the stopper in the drain. With what she had wanted to be a quick motion, she slowly bent over and gently tapped the stopper into place. The bath beads were already beginning to dissolve; foam was beginning to appear. She sat on the toilet, cover down, naked, touching her body, feeling the texture of her skin around her inner thighs. She remembered how taut and smooth it used to be. She remembered her husband gently kissing her in that very same spot, many, many years ago. She remembered what love was, and she cried.

The steam from the hot water fogged up the bathroom mirror, and wet beads of perspiration were beginning to slide off of her body too. For a minute, as she watched the tiny drops of water roll down the center of her chest, over her stomach, and down between her thighs, it felt as if her whole body was crying. Dripping, she got up and placed one foot at a time into the now half-filled bathtub, moving very slowly, until she was lying in the tub, her breasts and stomach floating out over the water, soaking in one huge pool of tears. And in this pool of tears, she rested.

❧

The steam rose from the pot in which she had placed the chicken breasts. It filled the apartment with the healing scent of chicken broth.

Lo voy a matar, she thought, and she cooked the mole for hours just as she had done so many times before.

When the mole was ready, she placed it in the Pyrex dish she bought at the supermarket and covered it with a piece of foil, securing it tightly along the edges for its long trip back to the other side.

"*Lo voy a matar*," she finally said out loud.

She looked through her bag for her favorite dress.

I'm going to look *bien bonita*, she thought as she stood in front of the bathroom mirror and put on a slip her husband had given her twelve years ago. It was the only gift he had ever given her during their entire marriage, and the only reason he had actually given her this gift was because her young son had bought it and given it to him to give to her for their anniversary. The delicate lace got caught on her left earring, and with a quick jerk, she yanked the slip down over her head. It was not until she looked in the mirror that she noticed the blood dripping; she had ripped her earring off, the tender lobe now cut in two. Immediately, she pinched the cut with one hand while she searched with the other for a Band-Aid in the medicine cabinet behind the mirror.

She said under her breath, over and over again, *"¡Lo voy a matar! Lo voy a matar! Lo voy a matar!"* From that moment on, it became her mantra.

She hadn't noticed the thunderstorm while in the apartment. She was so consumed with what she was about to do that she had no idea what was happening downtown until she arrived at the entrance to the bridge.

She found herself standing at the end of a long line to get onto the bridge, a Band-Aid on her ear, holding the foil-covered Pyrex dish gently with both her arms, as if it were a child.

When she put her money into the turnstile, a reporter shoved a microphone in front of her face and asked, "Have you seen the river, ma'am?"

"No," she answered. "What's a matter with the river? I don't know anything about it. What's a matter with the river?"

"Well, it's red, ma'am," the reporter told her.

"What do you mean, red?" she asked.

"Well, no one knows why, but the water of the river has turned red," said the reporter.

"Oh, my God!" exclaimed Estela. She tried to make the sign of the cross, but she couldn't because of the dish in her hands, and she absentmindedly pushed her way past the reporter to look at the river.

She could barely move, there were so many people. The dish almost fell out of her hands several times as people propelled her forward. Although she had now woken up somewhat from her reverie, her head was still spinning, and the mantra *¡Lo voy a matar!* was now playing over and over again in her head like a broken record. When she was finally able to make her way to the edge, she rested the dish on the rail and stared out into the clear, blue South Texas sky, not really noticing the color of the water. *¡Lo voy a matar!* was still ringing in her ears.

Staring down into the water blankly, her rage blinding her completely, she dripped with perspiration. The extreme heat and humidity caused her to pant. With the sudden, loud honk of an eighteen-wheeler, she awoke. The Pyrex dish slipped out of her hands, over the rail, into the red, red river. And as she turned, she saw two old men running across the bridge to help a young woman who was screaming.

Estela regained her composure, took a deep breath of the mulberry-scented air, and sighed. Covering her face with her hands, smelling a hint of mole and a whiff of poison under her fingernails, she said aloud, "*No lo voy a matar.*"

In the center of the pool table was a tiny tear, and that's what she was staring at, drunk. She had a little Virgen de Guadalupe tattooed on the back of her neck, but it was wrinkled like a sheet of paper that had gotten wet and had shriveled up as it dried.

A bright white pool ball slammed hard against the rail of the table, startling her. Her foot slipped off the homemade wrought iron rail that ran along the bottom of the bar. She was drunk and old. The ball slammed against the side, over and over again, returning to the young hustler's hand, like a yo-yo.

"*Oye*, Victor," she said to him. "How much you charge me to let me suck you?"

"You know I don't like to do it with old ladies, Perla," he answered. "Anyway, where's your boyfriend?"

"Shit," she slurred, "he can't even get it up anymore."

Victor just smiled.

"C'mon, Victor," she called again. "*Mira*," she said as she pulled out her false teeth. "*Tu no sabes* how this feels, baby." And she chewed on her old, pink gums, spreading her lips wide open, like a horse.

⁂

Several hours and ten beers later, Perla was completely drunk, sitting hunchbacked at a table, her head dangling over to the side, held on only by a skinny, wrinkled neck and the outspread hands of the Virgen de Guadalupe. She had been trying for half an hour to pick up a single grain of salt from the table, but she just couldn't do it. Finally, she licked her finger lightly and got the single grain of salt to stick. She tried to hold her hand steady over the glass of beer, but she couldn't stop it from shaking. She held it as steadily as she could and pushed the grain off her index finger with her thumb and watched it sink to the bottom of the glass, sending a tiny stream of bubbles to the top, where they popped, one by one, under her nose.

The cowboy boots slammed hard on the table, almost spilling her beer. She jerked, as if waking from a nightmare, and stared wide-eyed at the pair of boots directly in front of her. Nauseous, she tried to focus on the shiny, silver points at the tips of the boots but couldn't, her eyes bouncing uncontrollably to the heels and up the side of the boots, where the state of Texas and a bouquet of bluebonnets had been hand-tooled. Up, to the dark, hairy calves. Up, to the dark, hairy thighs. Up, to a bright red G-string, where she saw his hands come down to make the little red devil tattooed on his penis dance.

❧

When she finally stepped out into the hot South Texas sun that afternoon, she had to put one hand over her eyes to keep the light from blinding her and the other around the can of Budweiser she had snuck out of the bar to make sure it was still there inside her purse. She rested against the outside wall of the bar, at the corner, until she heard someone calling to her. She opened her eyes. The sky was dark and ominous, a city bus was waiting in front of her, the door open, and her old friend, Mateo, the bus driver, was yelling her name from the driver's seat.

"*Gracias*, Mateo," she said. "I was falling asleep."

"C'mon up, Perla," said the bus driver. "Hurry! It's gonna rain."

"Oh, thank you, Mateo," she said again, pulling herself up the first of the three steps into the bus. As she took the third and final step into the bus, she lost her grip and was about to fall backward when Mateo jumped out of the driver's seat to catch her. He made it just in time and helped her get on the bus and into the seat directly behind him. The bus immediately stank of alcohol, and just as immediately, she fell asleep, her face pressed against the window.

Mateo had been a bus driver for thirteen years, and every Friday, at exactly the same time, he stopped the bus at the same corner, opened the door, and called out at Perla to wake her from her drunken stupor. Every year, around Christmas, she'd give him a small package of tamales. For this he was truly grateful, and he always took special care of her when she was drunk.

She woke up as Mateo shook her gently.

"*¿Dónde estoy?*" she asked, wondering where she was.

"We're downtown," he said to her. "At the plaza. There was a huge storm. It rained a lot for a little while. There was no one left in the bus when it started raining. I thought that you should sleep."

"*Ay*, thank you, Mateo," she said to him, "You always take such good care of me. Why don't you find yourself a nice wife to take care of?"

"I think it's a little too late for that, Perla," he answered. "My marrying years have passed me by. Anyway, why do I need a wife to take care of when I have you?"

"*Ay*, Mateo." She continued, "What do you want with an old woman like me?"

"No, Perla," he said to her. "Look in the window. You're still beautiful."

"*Ay*, Mateo, may God make you a saint," she said. "Maybe you could become a priest. You know, you would be a very good priest."

"Perla." He asked as he chuckled, "Don't you have to meet Don Luis? It's already late in the afternoon."

"Oh, my God. You're right," she said, trying to make out the time on her watch through her drunk, sleepy eyes. "I better hurry. I was supposed to meet him an hour ago. *Dios te bendiga*, Mateo," she said to him as he helped her off the bus.

"Be careful, Perla," said the driver. "There's a whole lot of commotion going on over by the bridge. They say the river turned red or something. There's policemen and TV cameras and everything over there. I've been turning left on Convent all day long. They wouldn't let me go through. Be careful!"

She was in a hurry. She barely heard what he said as she began to cross the street toward the bridge. She had forgotten that she had to meet her husband on the Mexican side.

Several blocks away from the bridge, as she weaved from side to side, she ran into her old friend, Dora, who was also drunk.

"Hey, Perla," said Dora. "Have you seen the river?"

"No, Dora," said Perla. "How are you?"

"Oh, I'm fine, Perla," said Dora. "But go to the river right now! Hurry! Go running to see the river. It's red. They don't know what happen, but it's completely red, and they say it's a miracle. People are drinkin' the water, the red water, and the sick people are getting better. I don't know if it's true, mind you, but they say it's a miracle. Hurry! Go see. Go drink some water. I drank some to see if it'll stop me drinkin'. I don't know what to do anymore, so I drinked the water. We'll find out. Go, Perla! Go get some of the red water. I know you're tired of drinking too. Go!"

Perla said good-bye and began moving as quickly as she could toward the river. She really did not care about her own drinking problem, but if what they said was true, then she had to get some water for her little granddaughter who was born with a spinal defect. Perla remembered how the doctors had said that the child could never be cured. They were barely able to save her when they operated on her back a few days after she had been born to try and pack the spinal cord back under her skin. One of the doctors, the one from the American side, said that it was probably because Perla's daughter had drunk water from the tap during her pregnancy instead of the water from the plastic jugs. Perla didn't know what had caused the defect. Many times she blamed herself for being such a bad mother, never there when her daughter got home from school, never spending any time with her, always working until nine o'clock at night, and from work, straight to the bar. She really only saw her early in the morning, when she sent her off to school. Her daughter had practically raised herself, learning how to scramble eggs for dinner at the age of six. Perla was almost sure that it had been her fault that her granddaughter had been born with the defect. Maybe nothing had happened to her own daughter because of her drinking, but she knew that God was making her pay. When she wasn't drunk, which nowadays was almost never, she constantly prayed for her little granddaughter.

Then, from somewhere within her stupor, she found the presence of mind to go into Minimax Groceries one block away from the river and buy some string. As soon as she walked into the store, she saw the school supplies by the first checkout stand. She quickly grabbed a ball of mailing string, a large one, and waited in line for just a few minutes to pay for it. She ran out into the street to get in line to cross the bridge.

It took her about half an hour to get to the turnstile, and every few minutes, she'd pull the beer from her purse and take a sip. When she finally reached the bridge, there was only a little beer left in the can. She gulped it down as she put her quarter into the turnstile.

She had to push and shove her way to get to the bridge rail. When she got there, she stared into the river, praying as hard as she could for a miracle. She took the empty can from her purse and with difficulty tied the end of the string through the tab on the top of the can. Then, slowly she lowered the can a few inches at a time, from the bridge down into the red, red water, concentrating all of her attention on the can as it swayed in the hot, gentle South Texas breeze. When the can finally hit the surface of the water, she was almost out of string. She had to stand on her toes—drunk with alcohol, drunk with the thought of a miracle, drunk with Jesus—and lean precariously over the rail until the can filled with water.

She pulled on the string to make sure that the can was heavy with water and quickly towed it back up. Drunk as she was, she had a difficult time pulling on the string, and several times she almost lost her grip and the can. She prayed and prayed, with each and every tug, the entire time she pulled on the string until she could see the can through the bars of the railing. She took a deep breath and smelled the mulberries in the air mixed with alcohol.

When the can was finally within reach and she moved her hand over the railing to grab it, she was startled by the loud honk of an eighteen-wheeler, and she almost lost the can, but she was able to quickly slip the fingernail of her little finger into the beer tab and save it. She fell to the ground, exhausted, and closed her eyes for a second. When she opened them again, she saw a woman giving birth on the other side of the bridge.

Estoy soñando, she thought, thinking she was dreaming. And in her dream, she prayed for the child and her child and her child's child.

She felt cold suddenly, the hot breeze blowing across the perspiration on her skin. She smelled the bitter, pungent alcohol oozing from her pores as the sweet mulberries in the air soothed her into a deep, deep sleep.

7 lourdes

LOURDES found a dead man by the river. At that place where it's so wide, but you can still walk across it, waist-deep it is so shallow. He was lying there, dead, in a little, three-foot minivalley left by a stream that empties into the Rio Grande.

She saw "something shiny, red" beneath the dried-out shrubs at the mouth of the stream where it empties into the river. She saw it from far away. When she first turned the bend, the bright, South Texas sun made it really sparkle.

As she got closer, she saw the "something shiny" on a man's hand clutching the loose, sandy dirt at the river's edge as if to pull himself up. But he couldn't. Then she saw a white cuff, then a black suit.

In this heat? she thought.

She squatted down, poked the hand with a twig from the ground, then touched the stone on the ring with her forefinger. It frightened her, and she pulled back. But then, she slipped the ruby ring right off the dead man's finger, stood up, reached into her jeans, and slipped the ring into her panties, where it found its way down. Then she ran. She dropped her *chanclas*, which she had been holding in her hands while she had been wading at the river's edge.

She didn't even see his face. All she remembered was his arm sticking out like a small piece of driftwood, right here in her favorite grotto, where there was shade, where she could sit and think about why it was always too late for her.

But not this time! This time, she was there first.

She ran to the top of the steep hill, where the embankment of the river that floods once every fifty years met the street. And because she was so excited when she ran up to the street from the riverbed when she had discovered the dead man, she forgot that she had left her sandals behind, and the hot, hot pavement was now burning her feet, and a car was coming, and she was trying to get the driver's attention, and she was too excited to go back down and get her *chanclas* when she remembered. She flagged down a car and asked the driver to take her to the store down the road so that she could call the police.

⁂

The cop asked her as he looked down at the river from the top of the embankment, "What were you doing down there?"

"I was walking," she answered.

"Don't you know that's dangerous?" asked the policeman.

"No," she said, "I walk down there all the time. Early in the afternoon. I walk down to the river, over there, a little before it turns this way" —she pointed—"and then I walk all the way down behind to the *panadería* and get some sweet bread to eat with coffee. My mother likes it."

"But . . . ," said the policeman.

She interrupted, "Well, not all the time, you know. Only in the summer, when the sun goes down late; only when there's plenty of light. I never walk in the dark. In the winter"— she wouldn't stop talking—"in the winter, even though it doesn't get that cold, I don't walk down there. I stay up on the street. But it's boring. Sometimes I just don't come in the winter. If it's raining. Or cold. And we just eat raisin bread for *merienda*. With butter. Toasted sometimes. If the bread is brand new, we eat it soft. If it's a while old, we toast it. Me and my mother."

She was thirty-three years old. Not married anymore. Not divorced, though. He just left. Didn't get up one day and say, "I'm gonna go buy cigarettes," and never come back like any normal man would. No. He got up one day and said to Lourdes, "I'm leaving, and I'm never coming back." And he got in his truck, left, and never came back.

"She's been a little crazy ever since," she'd hear her mother whisper to others. (She thought her mother was crazy.)

She got a little fatter after that, but that was it, or so she thought.

"He can go to hell!" she had said after she finished crying.

"Have you been to Tano's Panadería?" she asked the policeman, who now had a ring of perspiration around his fat waist above the holster that fit too tight. "They have the best *regalos* in town. They put a lot of jelly in the middle, a lot, and the sugar, the melted sugar on top, is crusty, crispy-crunchy, very good, *esquisitos*," she said as she placed her finger to her lip. "Oh, and Tano, he likes the police. You can go. It's all right. The cops, they go there. They go there every day. He gives them free *pan dulce*. They watch the store. So go. Free sweet bread, *¡fíjate!*"

Another policeman came up the embankment onto the street. He was holding a wallet and some bills and some change and a pocket watch in his big, dark, sweaty hands.

"He's missing a finger," he said to the policeman talking to Lourdes.

Lourdes's eyes popped open wide.

"I mean," he corrected himself, giggling nervously from the find, "I mean he's missing a ring because the finger, it has a white line, you know, like a tan from the sun, like a ring is missing!"

"Why didn't you wait for the detectives?" asked the one cop angrily.

"I don't know. 'Cause I wanted to see, to look for ID. So I went in his pockets. I put on the gloves! What's wrong with that?" he countered.

"Go put them back. The detectives are going to be pissed off. Go put them back," he said to the rookie, and turned his head to talk to Lourdes. "You better not say anything about this, or I'll throw you in jail. Forever!"

"Oh no, sir," she said, her eyes still popped wide open, "I won't say a ting. I promise. I won't say a ting. I promise," feeling the ring inside her panties caught on a pubic hair, making her want to reach in and fix it or shift her legs or rub her thighs together or reach in and get it out and confess, holding the ring in her fingers, her hand out in front of her, falling to her knees:

"Here it is! *¡Aquí está! ¡Tómalo!* Take it! I don't want it. I just found him lying there, really. Here's the ring! *¡Tómalo!* Take it! It shined so pretty from far, far away, way over there where the river turns. I just grabbed it, but I didn't kill him! *No lo maté*! I'm sorry! I promise. I didn't kill him! Please don't take me to jail! I'm begging you. Please don't take me to jail!"

But she didn't. As much as she wanted to, she didn't confess. It was the first thing she had ever gotten first. It was the first time she wasn't too late. She reached down quickly and pushed it down a little when both policemen turned around to look at the detectives arriving in a big, unmarked, black car. She couldn't stand the itch anymore.

Finally beginning to get nervous, she thought, I shouldn't of taken it, and then, Too late!

"Who's this?" asked the detective as he got out of the car as if he were getting off a horse.

"She found him," said the policeman.

"Did you get her stats?" asked the detective.

"Yeah," answered the policeman.

"Let her go," he ordered.

"But aren't you gonna talk to her?" he asked.

"No, let her go," he answered.

"Are you sure?" insisted the cop.

"I said let her go!" yelled the detective.

"Okay, miss, you can go," said the policeman to Lourdes, and shook his head.

"Oh, really? Good!" she said, relieved. The ring was beginning to pinch her again.

"You can go. And don't walk down there anymore," he said to her, pointing toward the river.

"No, sir," she said. "I won't. Don't worry. I'm gonna go buy the sweet bread. Don't worry." And she started walking up the street to the bakery.

Suddenly she turned around but continued walking backward and said to the policeman, "Listen, sir, some see a stick, some see a snake. Me, I see nothing."

He looked at her and said in his fat white boy accent, "*Loca*, lady. You're *loca*, lady," and grinned.

She continued walking up the street, being careful not to bring her hands anywhere near her crotch so as to not bring any attention to herself or the ring, although she was dying to because the prongs that held the ruby kept getting caught in her hair and pulling, and she was nervous that there would be cops getting sweet bread at the bakery. She was really nervous, and it was so hot, so, so hot.

The bakery's old, dilapidated screen door got stuck at the top every time Lourdes pulled on the handle. The door would twist at the center, the bottom would pull out, and then the top corner would finally give way with a snap that always hit her. No matter how careful she was opening the door, it always hit her, and today it hit her on the forehead, hard.

"¿Oiga, Tano, cuándo va a componer la puerta?" she asked the old man behind the counter. "It hit me hard. Really hard." She rubbed her forehead just above her left eye.

"*Ay, mija*, I'm sorry. I don't want to fix it. I'm tired. Be careful when you come in. That's why I put the little bells!" he said to her, feeling truly sorry.

The door had hit her so hard, she didn't even hear the bells.

"What do you want, *mija*?" he asked her tenderly.

"*Lo mismo de siempre*," she answered.

Then she remembered when she felt another tug down there. She got nervous again, thinking about what she had done.

It wasn't so bad, she thought. He was dead. I got there first. Oh, my God, it's hot in here. And it was. It was even hotter than outside—so much heat from the stoves.

Tano wore Coke bottle glasses. A perfect circle in the middle of each lens, like a magnifying glass, made the center of his eyes look huge, like a character in Dick Tracy.

"*¿Y cómo está tu mamá?*" he asked Lourdes.

"*Muy bien,* Don Tano, *ella está muy bien!*"

Tano slid the glass doors of the wood and glass vitrine open and pulled out two *regalos*. The glass top of the vitrine was scratched to a smooth, even opaqueness from all the nickels, dimes, and pennies that had touched it over the fifty or more years of the bakery's existence. Lourdes, bending a bit, followed him from the other side of the vitrine as he pulled out the sweet bread. He grabbed the first two pieces of bread with long, rusty tongs and dropped them into a small paper bag. The itch in her panties was now unbearable, and she asked the old man to put two *marranitos* in a separate bag—she had a plan. When he turned around to get another bag, she pushed her pelvis into the glass panel to try and dislodge the ring. She stood there grinding her pelvis into the glass case while he fiddled, opening the bag. And finally she was relieved.

The little bells on the screen door rang, and then the door slammed shut. It was a cop coming for his free bread.

Lourdes got nervous. She paid for her bread as Don Tano said hello to the policeman, stepped quickly out of the bakery, and started her long walk home.

The following day around noon, Lourdes woke up in a cold sweat, exhausted. The heat and the dead man were driving her crazy—she couldn't get either of them out of her mind. The water cooler in her window made everything worse, getting everything damp. She had barely slept an hour all night, thinking. When she did lapse into sleep, the dead man's hand would wake her—nudge her from her sleep. All she could feel was the heat. And then she'd wake up covered in perspiration.

Dead tired, she reached under the mattress, where she had hidden the ring last night. It was still there.

She jumped out of bed, grabbed the bottle of Holy Water from her tiny altar on the armoire, and cupped the ring in her hand while she drowned it in Holy Water with the other, praying out loud.

She held the top of the bottle of Holy Water, dropped the ring inside, put the top back on, and hid the bottle back under the mattress. Then she went to the bathroom and showered in cold, cold water.

Oh, my God! *¡Diosito Santo!* Oh, my God! *¡Diosito Santo!* Oh, my God! *¡Diosito Santo!* she thought as she stepped out of the shower, fear finally completely taking over her.

Her hair still wet from the shower, she stepped into the living room, where her mother had fallen asleep in her favorite chair. Just as she was about to walk out the door, her mother called, "Lourdes?"

"*Sí, Mamá*," she answered.

"¿A dónde vas?" asked the mother.

"I'm goin' downtown, Mom," she said, holding a large, brown paper bag out in front of her to show her mother. "I'm gonna go eschange this dress I bought for little Gela's birthday gift. I asked Petra what size she was, and she told me that Gela wears toddler, not one-year-old. So I have to eschange it. I'll be back *al ratito*."

There was no dress in the bag. She had taken the bottle of Holy Water, the ring still in it, and wrapped it in the doily her mother had knit for her altar and had had blessed by the Monsignor at St. Anne's.

"Is it pretty, *mija*?" asked Lourdes' mother. "Let me see it."

"No, Mother," she answered. "I'm in a hurry. The dress was on sale, and I want to get to the store right away 'cause someone's gonna buy the size I need. I'll be home in a few hours, Mom."

"Okay, *mija*," she said to Lourdes. "*Ten cuidado*."

Her heart was pounding as she closed the door behind her. She clutched the bag desperately, thinking, What do I do with it? Where do I throw it? What do I do with it? Where do I throw it? Where do I throw it?

She couldn't go back to where she found the dead man, or they'd find her, the cops.

She said to herself, "*¡Diosito Santo!* Oh, my God!"

Not knowing what to do, she stayed on the bus until it made its last stop, at the main plaza in front of Rexall Drugs. It was pouring rain, out of nowhere. An old lady was asleep on the seat across the aisle from her, and Lourdes nudged her when she started to get off the bus to let her know that the bus was at its last stop.

The driver turned around and said to her, "No, don't wake her up. I'm gonna let her sleep for a little while. She's tired."

Lourdes nodded a thank-you to the driver and made her way to the door. She held the paper bag over her head as if it could protect her from the thunderstorm.

She rounded the corner at Iturbide and Convent and ran under the canopy of the Rialto Theater to get out of the rain. There were policemen everywhere. News cameras. Armed National Guardsmen. And people, lots of people everywhere. Then she got scared. Because she felt so guilty, she thought for a split second that the policemen were looking for her—and the ring. But then she heard two old ladies talking by the ticket booth. "No, Maria, it's not another revolution, don't worry. The river turned red." Maria gasped. "They don't know why, but it's red, as red as *aqua de sandía. ¡Fíjate!* Don't go over there, Maria. There's too many people. I can't walk anymore either. When you get older, your knees go. That was the first thing that went with me . . . ," she continued.

Lourdes started walking toward the bridge in the rain; she no longer cared if she got wet.

"The river is red. The river is red," she kept saying to herself over and over again. "It's the dead man's blood and this ring. Red. Red like the ruby on it. Yes, it's the dead man's blood and his ruby ring that I took that turned the river red. Oh, my God! *¡Diosito Santo!*"

She pushed her way to the turnstile and through the crowd gathered at the edge of the bridge.

"Oh, my God! They're gonna see me. How do I do this?" she asked herself as she clutched the brown bag to her chest.

Lourdes was pushed up against the railing right at the entrance to the bridge by the throng. She had never been anywhere so crowded before in her life. She couldn't breathe. She felt like pushing her way out of the crowd and running back home. She couldn't believe it when she saw the Rio Grande red as blood, ruby red.

She pushed the paper bag down where she was sure no one could see it and reached in to grab the bottle of Holy Water that held the ruby ring. She was sure everyone was looking at her, but actually nobody cared. They were all looking at the river. She pulled the plastic bottle out of the bag, dropped it to the sidewalk next to her feet, and kicked it under the rail into the river.

Without even looking to see if the bottle fell into the river, she turned around and pushed her way through the crowd and walked back to the American side. She boarded the bus in front of the JC Penney on Convent and headed back home. The bottle of Holy Water and the ruby ring floated down the red, red Rio Grande, bobbing up and down on the river's surface like a fishing float. No one even noticed.

HER fingers were swollen where the rope that held the box together rubbed against them. Farmworkers were protesting on the plaza in front of the Presidential Palace, where she got the metro. She was not wearing any jewelry because she was thinking of a story that she read last night in the newspaper—an old woman, just like herself, had had her finger chopped off for a simple band of gold.

She was pushed onto the train by what seemed a hundred people until her cheek was pressed against the window of the door on the opposite side. She heard the conductor's buzzer announcing the closing of the doors, and she shuddered, remembering the old lady and her finger.

The train started moving, and she heard the sweet music of a bamboo flute and a tin can drum coming from the other side of the train. Then she heard a child's voice singing, in Nahuatl—she thought. Packed into the train, barely able to breathe, she felt as if she was going to faint. Out of the eye that was pressed against the window, she saw a bright green train speed by. Then a blue train, faster. Then a red train, faster and faster—until she felt she was flying through the tunnel, the music humming her along.

After what seemed a long time, the train stopped suddenly, and with it, the music. Five stories underground at the Chapultepec Park station, her cheeks were wet with tears, her arms asleep, one hand glued to the rail above her, the other now numbed beyond pain by the rope.

She needed desperately to get off the train, the brittle rope finally making her fingers bleed. She pushed her way to the door and stopped suddenly; she couldn't see because of the tears pouring uncontrollably from her eyes. At the door, she accidentally hit something with her foot. On the cement floor in front of her, a man was sliding along, pulling himself onto the train, no legs, but big, deformed, muscular arms. She wasn't sure that she was awake, but she did what she could to take a sleepwalker's step to get out of his way.

Walking straight ahead in a daze, she fell to the ground at the base of a huge flight of stairs.

The box crashed to the floor, glass breaking, honey running everywhere, mixing with the blood from her fingers. She found the strength to pull herself up, grabbing the base of the handrail with the hand that wasn't torn, and looked up the stairs as if she were at the foot of a huge pyramid. She prayed as if she'd never prayed before, to the Virgen de Guadalupe, to Quetzalcoatl, to Jesus—to anyone who was listening—for a wooden board with wheels.

She knew that she was going to die. She didn't know how or where, but she knew. She realized why she had come to Mexico City the second she arrived here. It was because she wanted to remember. She wanted to see La Montaña Rusa at Chapultepec Park. She wanted to go to that tiny yarn store on Insurgentes and buy one of those gigantic balls of silk yarn to knit her shroud. She just couldn't get the roller coaster and the giant ball of yarn out of her head.

And here she was in Mexico City, in a pool of honey, feeling faint. She started to laugh as she thought about her situation and how silly she felt for falling. Pura wiped tears away with her hands, smearing honey all over her face at the same time, the sweetness making its way with the salty tears onto her lips, into her mouth, making her laugh even more with the taste of it. She struggled to her feet. It took her quite a while. And still, as if on a pilgrimage, she began to climb the stairs, one by one, saying the name of a different saint with every step. It took her almost an hour to reach the top; some children helped her for a while. She talked with them and made them laugh.

"It's just that I'm so fat," she said to them in Spanish every three or four steps, and they giggled.

"I don't know what an old, fat lady like me is doing in Mexico City, carrying that stupid, heavy box of jars full of honey all by myself. But no! As soon as that lady gave some to me on a piece of bread, oh, I was in heaven. So I bought them. Like an idiot. Oh, I'm an idiot," she said to the children, but this time in English, and again, they laughed even though they could not understand.

"What was I thinking of?" she asked herself as she reached the top, and then she answered herself matter-of-factly, "Death."

She had woken up one morning back home and, for no apparent reason, had walked across Martin Plaza to the travel agency at the Washington Hotel and told the young woman sitting behind the desk that she needed a ticket to Mexico City. And so, the following day, early in the morning, she got her ticket and called for a cab to pick her up at "the old folks' home." She packed a couple of dresses, some underwear, her toothbrush, and her Florida water in a small faux leather bag she had ordered recently from the TV shopping network.

The following morning, she awoke to the trumpets of the soldiers raising the flag in front of the Presidential Palace and walked to the metro station on the east side of the Zócalo to make her way to Chapultepec Park to look at the "world's largest roller coaster" and buy her ball of yarn.

Satisfied, ball of yarn in her shopping bag, one jar of honey left in her purse from the accident, and "the world's largest roller coaster" in her head, she was ready to go back to her little city by the river.

⁂

She boarded the plane back to the border. As soon as the flight attendant helped her strap herself into her seat, she fell asleep. She had those magic little pills her doctor had prescribed for her so that she could sleep at night. Since she knew that the flight would make her nervous, she placed a pill under her tongue and smiled a thank-you at the flight attendant when she handed her a pillow.

The flight was uneventful. She woke up when the flight attendant gently nudged her shoulder and handed her a small plastic dish with half a cheese sandwich, half a ham sandwich, and two or three little pickles.

"Oh, thank you," she said as she pulled the tray down from the back of the seat in front of her.

As soon as the flight attendant had served her her Coca-Cola, Pura yelled because the plane hit an air pocket. Her sandwich flew up in the air, and Pura began to laugh out loud. She had such a beautiful laugh that the flight attendant started laughing too, and before they knew it, everyone in the airplane seemed to be laughing. The flight attendant picked up the cheese sandwich that had fallen in the aisle, took Pura's plate, and pulled another out from under the cart to hand to her. But as she handed Pura the new dish, she noticed water dripping from the ceiling, from under the storage bins.

After a few minutes, the pilot's voice came over the intercom, asking everyone to fasten their seat belts. He said that the water was due to a slight problem with the cabin pressure, but that there was nothing to worry about. He then instructed all the flight attendants to fasten themselves into their little seats that came out of the wall at the front and the back of the airplane. He informed the passengers that there might still be some turbulence up ahead. Pura began to get nervous. She felt her heart beating faster as she noticed the water continuing to drip from the ceiling.

Pura was not the only one on the plane who was concerned about the water. The alarm buttons were ringing and blinking throughout the plane. All of a sudden, it took another dip, and everyone screamed.

The captain's voice came over the speaker again, reminding them that there was nothing wrong, that the jolt had simply been caused by an air pocket, and that they were only about forty-five minutes from the border.

Pura's heart began to race again, and it beat even faster when she saw the pilot emerging from the cockpit to inspect the situation. By now, almost everyone was alarmed, and the pilot assured them, row by row, that nothing was wrong. This made her think that something was wrong. She was beginning to get very wet, as was everyone else. It seemed as if it was drizzling inside the plane. She began to feel faint.

The pilot returned to the cockpit, and as soon as he had closed the door behind him, the plane took another dip, this one so intense that some of the overhead compartments popped open, and luggage fell into the aisles; luckily, no one was hit.

The oxygen masks fell from their hideaways above the passengers, and the pilot spoke again, instructing passengers to use the oxygen if they felt they needed it. Pura felt a sharp, sudden pain in her chest.

She thought, This is it. I'm going to die, and her head fell gently to the side as if she had fallen asleep.

The flight attendant, who had been keeping her eye on Pura because she reminded her of her own grandmother, noticed Pura's head falling to the side. She unbuckled her belt and hurried toward her. She nudged her gently as she had done when she woke her up to offer her a meal but got no reaction. She knew something was wrong. Quickly, she walked to the front of the plane and stepped into the cockpit.

Before she came back out, the captain was on the intercom, asking, "Is there a doctor on the plane? If there is a doctor on the plane, please come to the front."

Two men rose from their seats. They looked at each other and questioned if they should both go. They nodded at each other and began to walk toward the cockpit. But before they got to the front, the flight attendant came out of the cockpit and whispered to them in Spanish, "I have an old lady in row twenty-eight who seems to have fainted, and I'm worried about her because she did not answer me when I went to see if she was all right. Would either of you please take a look at her? She's very nice, and I'm really worried."

"Certainly," said both doctors, and followed the flight attendant down the aisle.

One of the doctors went to his seat to get his medical bag. The other doctor reached into his pocket and pulled out what seemed to be a very small flashlight. He examined Pura's eyes. When the other doctor returned, the doctor who was attending to Pura told him that she had fainted, but that after taking her pulse, he was afraid that she might have heart problems. The flight attendant did her best to hold back her tears, but one escaped. She knew that she should not show any emotion so as not to excite the other passengers. One of the doctors pulled out a small glass tube from his bag, wrapped it in gauze, snapped it in half, and placed it under Pura's nose. Pura reacted immediately, tossing her head, coming to. A big smile came over the flight attendant's face.

After a while, drenched in both her own perspiration and the dripping water, Pura told the doctors that she had had a sharp pain in her chest and that that was the last thing she remembered. One of the doctors asked her if she took any medication. She said that she took some "little white pills" for her heart and that she had some in her purse. The flight attendant pulled the purse from under the seat and handed it to Pura. When she showed the bottle to the doctors, they agreed that she had probably had a mild heart attack. The doctor instructed her to take one of her pills, and as he did so, the pilot's voice came over the speaker, again instructing everyone to take their seats and fasten their seat belts because the plane was beginning to make its final descent into the city.

By now, without explanation, the rain inside the plane was beginning to subside. A few drops still trailed down the windows on the left side. One of the doctors suggested to the flight attendant that she call for an ambulance. She told him that she would do so immediately. She told Pura that it would be waiting for her when she got to the airport.

Pura asserted, "*¡Claro que no!*"

Pura said she felt a lot better and that even if the flight attendant called an ambulance, she was going to refuse to get into it. And to prove that she was okay, Pura unbuckled her seat belt and began to get up. The flight attendant asked her to please sit down and assured her that she would not call an ambulance.

"If you are anything like my grandmother, you will refuse to get into the ambulance," the flight attendant said to Pura, and smiled.

Pura smiled back.

"Please thank those two handsome young doctors for me," she said to the flight attendant, and continued, "Are you married?"

The fight attendant answered, "No."

Pura continued, "Well, honey, you should talk to the young doctor, the one with the mustache. He is very handsome, and he's not married. I looked at his hand, and he wasn't wearing a ring!"

The flight attendant blushed and gently touched Pura on the cheek.

"I hope you feel better," she said to Pura. "I'll personally take you into the terminal, but you have to promise me that you'll let me take you in a wheelchair."

"Absolutely not," answered Pura. "I walked onto this flying rainstorm, and I'm going to walk off of it."

The flight attendant understood who she was dealing with and that there would be no way that this beautiful old lady would allow herself to be wheeled into the terminal. She told Pura to call her if she needed anything and walked to her seat to strap herself in for the landing.

⁂

Inside the terminal, the flight attendant asked Pura if there was someone waiting for her. Pura answered, "No, *hija*, I'm all alone. Nobody left. Would you please help me get a taxi?"

The flight attendant answered, "Of course."

As she was about to get into the cab, Pura reached into her purse and gave the flight attendant the only jar of honey she had left.

She said, "Here, take this. I'm fat enough already. Be careful in those crazy airplanes. And eat a little spoonful of this honey when you want your life to be a little sweeter. But not too much, huh, or you'll get big and fat like me." She laughed her beautiful laugh.

The flight attendant smiled, thanked her, closed the car door, and waved as the taxi sped off toward the highway.

"How's the traffic on the bridge?" Pura asked the cabdriver.

"Oh, it's terrible with everything that's going on down there," said the taxi driver.

"What's going on down there?" she asked.

"You haven't heard?" asked the driver. "The river turned red. No one knows what happened. They think it's a chemical or something. I think it's a miracle."

"Oh, my God," said Pura softly to herself. "Is the world coming to an end?"

"I won't even be able to take you but maybe as close as two or three blocks from the bridge. You are not going to believe the people, TV cameras, reporters, helicopters. I even saw a blimp, the same one from the football games, flying around the bridge earlier today. I'm sorry, señora," said the driver.

"Oh, don't worry, son," Pura said in Spanish. "Just get me as close as you can. I'll walk the rest of the way. Usually I wouldn't even mind. It's just that, you see, I'm so fat, and I felt a little sick on the airplane. But it doesn't matter; just get me as close as you can."

"*Sí, señora,*" said the taxi driver, and continued, "I'm going to turn on the radio for you so you can hear what's going on down there."

"*Gracias, hijo,*" Pura replied, and smiled sweetly.

The taxi driver was only able to get as close as four blocks from the bridge. He explained to Pura that if he got any closer, he'd be stuck there all day, and he really needed to keep working; he really needed the money just to make ends meet.

"Otherwise," he said, "I'd take you all the way to the other side and drop you off right at the door of your house."

"Oh, don't worry, *hijo,*" she said. "This is good enough. I'll walk the rest of the way," and she handed him five extra dollars.

He refused to take the money, but she insisted, and after grabbing her purse and her shopping bag, she closed the car door and waved.

It was hot, so, so hot. She began to perspire as soon as she stepped out of the air-conditioned cab, a cold, cold sweat. With every step she took, she felt weaker, and when she was finally able to see the bridge, she felt as if she was going to faint. She stopped at a fruit stand

and ate a piece of watermelon to refresh herself. She felt better and decided to battle the crowd. By the time she was able to push her way to the tollbooth, she knew that she was really ill. She began to feel the pain in her chest again, and as she stepped onto the bridge, she took the plastic bottle from her purse and placed one of the little white pills under her tongue. She pushed her way to the rail to hold herself up and was completely startled when she saw the red water.

Short of breath, Pura began to pant, but she still noticed the strange scent of mulberries in the air. The smell was so familiar! As a child, growing up in a small house close to the river, she and her little sister used to make mulberry mud pies and bake them in the miniature sandstone oven their father had built for them. An eighteen-wheeler honked, and the shock made her heart beat even faster, intensifying the pain. She held on to the rail tightly; she felt as if her heart were exploding.

Suddenly the pain stopped, her legs went weak, she slid down slowly, almost gently, against the rail, down to the cement sidewalk, closed her eyes, took one last deep breath of mulberries, and died. The big ball of white yarn rolled out of her shopping bag and fell into the red, red Rio Grande.

9

cristina

"YOU have to know *how* to eat a tortilla chip or you'll cut your mouth," Cristina said to the group of tourists she was leading through the old Capitol of the Republic of the Rio Grande, where she worked part-time while she finished her degree in criminal justice. She had just pointed out the old stone *metate* sitting in the corner of the hundred-and-fifty-year-old kitchen.

"In those days," she said—she started every sentence of her hourly routine with "in those days"—"the women would buy the corn the day before and soak it in a pail with lime overnight, not the lime like a lemon but a lime like a powder, so that in the morning, before the men woke up, they could put the softened corn on that thing"—she pointed to the old *metate*—"and ground it up until they made the masa, the dough for making the corn tortillas.

"Now, you may ask me, 'What does eating a corn tortilla chip have to do with cutting your mouth?'" she said, looking at them as if waiting for a response, "but the truth is that in those days, if you took the tortilla chip that your wife had just fried up for you good and hard, crispy hard for you and bit into it like this"—she placed her fingers up to her mouth as if she were holding a chip vertically—"instead of like this"—she held her fingers to her mouth as if she were holding the tortilla chip horizontally—"then the tip of the tortilla chip, you know, the triangle, the tip of the triangle, would poke you on the top of your mouth, and you would get an infection. And the nearest doctor was in Monterrey or San Antonio, 165 miles away, so you would die.

"So be careful," she continued, "when you go to the other side of the river into Mexico. Remember to hold your tortilla chip like this, not like this, when you bite it," and she let out a wild, raw guffaw.

The tourists stood there in the old stone house, perspiring, staring directly at Cristina with absolutely no idea what she was talking about—except that they might die in Mexico.

She stood in front of the cloudy mirror that hung from a square-head nail on the wall of the bathroom where the people who once lived here used to wash. Staring intently at the mirror, she noticed the tiny, little lines beginning to form from the corners of her eyes.

She said to herself, "I need the Retin A!"

Taking a few steps back and holding up her blouse, she pinched a good three inches of her belly and thought, I need the diet pills.

Cristina tucked her blouse back into her tight-fitting skirt, smoothing it down over her love handles, and thought, I'm really hungry. I'm gonna go across the river and get a corn. Corn's not fattening. I'll get it plain, with only salt and lime. Minina told me to eat lots of vegetables. Corn's a vegetable, right? No . . . Yes . . . No, they make cereal with corn; it can't be a vegetable. No, yes, it is. *Ay Dios*, tomorrow I'll start my diet.

She stepped out of the bathroom and headed for the front desk to grab her purse. She said to the old man who helped her, "Paulino, take your lunch break. The rain stopped an hour ago. I'm gonna go out for a while now. C'mon, Paulino, I have to lock the door," and she pushed him out, locking the heavy wooden doors of the old Capitol of the Republic of the Rio Grande with the huge, old metal skeleton key. She dropped it in her purse.

She was dying to see the river. Her friends who worked at the stores downtown had been dropping by all day to tell her about the color and all the commotion going on just a few blocks from where she worked. But she had been busy with tour after tour—especially after the downpour—the Anglo tourists seemed to come in off the street simply to get out of the rain.

I'm so tired of repeating this same damn speech over and over, and I'm too tired to study for that damn test in political science tonight. I'm so damn stressed out, she thought as she stepped out of the tiny museum.

Inspired by a cop show on TV about the Dallas police detectives who investigated the Kennedy assassination, she had decided three years ago to become a policewoman, a detective, hopefully. Now she was already a junior public justice major—barely passing her classes, but just one more year, and she would graduate. Then the police academy. Ever since that TV show, she became obsessed with conspiracies, and she had read every book about every Kennedy assassination plot she could get her hands on. And she had found a lot of information and misinformation on the Internet too.

The second she could see Convent, she knew that something was the matter.

She saw the National Guard out in force, policemen everywhere, even members of the other armed forces, and then, as she turned the corner, from far away, she noticed the Mexican special police, the Federales, in their black outfits, all over the Mexican side of the bridge. "I'm gonna get to the bottom of this," she said to herself, "something's very smelly in the state of Texas," misquoting Shakespeare from last semester's Lit class as the scent of mulberries hit her, and she sniffed the air, her nose pointed up, like a hound dog.

Cristina pushed her way through the crowd to the center of the bridge and stood there, right in the middle, tapping her fingers on the rail, trying to "solve the case."

She was starving, yet she completely forgot about the corn on the cob she was going to eat and didn't even cross to the Mexican side to get it. She began to walk back to the American side with a mission and turned around suddenly when she heard an eighteen-wheeler screech to a halt. A bunch of people were screaming. Her adrenaline pumping, she continued walking fast, imagining that the Federales were about to let go with a round of machine-gun bullets. She quickened her pace, walking right past a woman giving birth without even noticing. She was so concerned with the color of the river and who or what might be behind it that probably partly out of fear, she marched double time toward the American side. She saw nothing but soldiers, policemen, and special agents. She couldn't understand the smell of mulberries all around her, and anything she did not understand became part of the "conspiracy."

Cristina frowned.

She never went back to work that day. She went straight home and immediately telephoned her cousin, Ernie, who worked at Shelley Air Force Base, air reconnaissance expert, computer whiz, and militant Chicano. He told her that he knew about what was happening on the border. As a matter of fact, he told her that he had just seen the first aerial photos of the river. "It's a bright, bright red from just west of the city almost all the way to the Gulf of Mexico," he said to her over the phone.

She convinced him to send the photo to the newspapers. "So that everybody, even the world, will know what the government is doing to our people. Viva La Raza!"

Within minutes, he e-mailed the photograph to the *San Antonio Express News*, making the transmission untraceable. The following morning, the photo was on the front page of every newspaper around the world. At night, Cristina, dressed all in black, snuck to the banks of the Rio Grande and filled a mayonnaise jar with the red water, packed it in a box, and sent it under an assumed name via Greyhound to her cousin in San Antonio. He had some friends in the bacterial warfare laboratories of one of the other bases in the city. They promised to analyze the water. "I'll send the results to every damn newspaper in the country," he told Cristina. "¡*Viva* La Raza!"

But on the first bump the bus hit, the jar broke.

"They held the bus at the checkpoint for more than two hours. The German shepherds went crazy from the smell. What'd you have in there, son? Was your momma sending you some jam?" the old black porter at the Greyhound bus station asked him as he handed him a soft, soggy, dark red cardboard box that had been torn apart, inspected, and stuffed into a plastic bag.

*

Cristina sat at home on her old, plastic-covered, green couch that evening after returning from the Greyhound bus station and watched David Letterman on TV.

At the beginning of his monologue, Letterman said, "We've all heard about all that commotion going on down there in the Rio Grande. You know, the river turned red, and all of the government officials down there still can't tell us exactly what is happening. There is, however, one woman down there who says she knows what's happening. She says that the water turned red by an act of God. That's right. That it's a miracle. Well, I think it's a miracle too!"

The audience laughed and cheered.

He continued, "This woman in South Texas, I believe her name is Cindy. Is that right, Biff?" he asked someone on the other side of the camera.

"Yes, Cindy," answered the man.

"Well, this woman, Cindy, she says that when she drank some of the red water from the river, her front tooth, which had fallen out, miraculously grew back right there on the bridge," continued Letterman.

The audience yelled, laughed, and cheered again.

"Well, we have a special treat for you tonight, thanks to our CBS affiliate down on the border. Take a look at the monitors," he said, pointing at a close-up of Cindy, kneeling on the bridge, pointing at her mouth, the new tooth in the front of her mouth blackened out.

"Before . . . ," continued Letterman, and pointed again at the same photo of Cindy on the TV screen, this time her brand-new sparkling white tooth glowing on the screen, " . . . and after."

The audience laughed hysterically.

"Before . . . and after," he repeated over and over again, showing one picture after the other, one picture after the other, until the audience was laughing and clapping again. "Before . . . and after. Before . . . and after."

Cristina thought, This is a big deal. This is a very big conspiracy.

The program was suddenly interrupted by a flashing Special Report sign. A bird's-eye view of the bridge flashed onto the screen; the red

Rio Grande flowing under it was lit bright as daylight by the helicopter's powerful searchlights, a red so rich, it looked like blood. The loud, chopping noise of the helicopter's blades suddenly exploded out of the small television set, as if she had accidentally sat on the volume control button of the remote. There was no other sound except for the sound of the helicopter's blades. Cindy kept waiting for the TV's volume to go back down to its regular level or for the broadcaster's voice to come through, but there was obviously a problem with the audio. The blaring sound of the swishing blades immobilized her. She couldn't even reach for the remote on the coffee table right in front of her to lower the volume. She was mesmerized.

It was as if she were there, on the bridge, under the helicopter, feeling its hot wind, the strong scent of mulberries she had smelled that afternoon, looking down over the rail into the red, red waters of the Rio Grande.

WHEN she was a little girl, she was blinded in the left eye by a kernel of popcorn as she peeked under the cover of the pan. It had a thick, milky-white coating all around it, the eye, and this is how she saw the world—milky, thick, and white. She knew then that she had been born to suffer.

She spent all afternoon, Sunday, the weekend of her First Holy Communion, collecting some sort of freshwater clams at Falcon Lake, southeast of the city. By evening, when everyone was packing up into the car, she held her giant Ziploc freezer bag full of clams, some large like fifty-cent pieces, some tiny like dimes.

When the family got home, something happened to Rosa that changed her life, one of two occurrences that same year. She went outside under the corrugated tin roof that served as a party tent for the Sunday afternoon barbecues during the long, hot, South Texas summers and as a garage for the mustard-yellow Dodge Duster her dad drove her to school in in the mornings. She set the pail right under the light-bulb that hung next to the No Pest strip that had been there since 1966 in the middle of the tin roof, filled the pail with water from the spigot next to the Japanese apple tree, and dumped her clams into it. Then she went into the kitchen and snuck a knife out of a drawer, unaware that her mother was watching her out of the corner of her eye but said nothing. As soon as she left, her older brother ran from behind the big, brick barbecue grill and fiddled with the clams, constantly looking toward the kitchen door to make sure Rosa wouldn't see him. When she finally came back, kitchen knife in hand, she picked the clams up, one at a time, and pried the shells open. At exactly clam number thirty-seven, she began screaming and yelling. Inside the house, her mother immediately imagined the sharp knife piercing the palm of Rosa's hand or a finger being cut off, but it was no such thing. Rosa had found a pearl.

The uncles and aunts who had been at the picnic rushed into the kitchen to see the pearl. The smart uncle said it was impossible, that only oysters made pearls. But everybody stared in amazement when Rosa pulled the fat pearl out of the tiny shell.

Rosa had just read in school the parable in which Jesus multiplied the fishes and loaves to feed those who had gathered to hear him speak, and so she immediately made some strange connection between the parable and the pearl—she knew it was a miracle, and she began to pray silently in her head.

Behind the green door that led from the kitchen to the grandmother's bedroom, Rosa's brother giggled, holding the string of fake pearls he had taken from the tin box in which the grandmother kept her buttons.

From that day forward, Rosa waited for more signs from God.

And she got one the following summer, when she would not stop talking about the story of the apparition of Our Lady of Guadalupe to Juan Diego. Every day, after school, for more than a week, she would tell and retell the story to everyone in the family. How Juan Diego had been so good that the Virgin had appeared to him on a hill in the heart of Mexico City and had given him roses, completely out of season in the winter, to take back to the Bishop as proof.

She knew now for sure that the pearl she found in that clam had been her roses—her proof of the existence of God.

On a Friday afternoon, she went outside and sat under the Japanese apple tree to play with her dolls. All at once, a deluge of rose petals floated down softly from the sky. She stared up in disbelief into the hot, bright, South Texas sun with her milky eye and thought for a split second that she saw God on a cloud. She gathered the rose petals into her skirt and ran inside, crying. She knelt in front of her grandmother, who was reading a novella in the big, turquoise, plastic-covered chair, and dumped the rose petals at her feet.

Her older brother climbed down carefully from the corrugated tin roof next to the Japanese apple tree, sliding down one of the six galvanized steel poles that held the tin roof up. He held a plastic bucket in one hand while he slid down, holding the pole with the other. Two or three dark red rose petals were stuck to the bottom of the bucket.

No one believed her, of course.

Her father almost forced her mother to take her out of Catholic School, saying, "It's those crazy nuns that are making her think that she's a saint. You better get her out of that school *antes que esas monjas la vuelvan loca.*"

The mother put her foot down, saying, "I'm not taking her out of that school, and that's that!"

Her father was convinced the nuns would eventually drive Rosa crazy. "If they haven't already!"

⁂

Many years later, fifteen years old, now almost out of high school and so smart, Rosa sat under the same Japanese apple tree on an extremely hot summer afternoon, cross-legged, staring at the sun with her milky eye, perspiring, when the sky suddenly turned a dark, dark gray.

She felt her sign was coming.

That afternoon, after the torrent had subsided, she saw the news about the river on TV. She stared intently at the new television set. She stared at the news of the dark, dark red river.

"Just like the color of the roses that fell on me from heaven," she whispered to herself.

She cried, put on her white patent-leather shoes and her favorite white cotton summer dress, and, without telling anyone, let the screen door slam shut behind her. She headed for the bridge.

She broke several roses from a bush in a neighbor's front yard. She didn't feel the thorns; she was looking for God. She only had to walk about twelve blocks before she was on Convent, looking south.

Three blocks from the bridge she broke out in song. One song after the other from the back of the prayer book at church.

"Eat his body, drink his blood, and we'll sing a song of love. Allelu! Allelu! Allelu! Alleluia!" sang Rosa, walking slowly toward the bridge, holding the flowers in front of her.

People stared.

"*Está loca,*" they were saying. But she wasn't crazy. She was looking for God.

As crowded as the hot streets were, people parted as she walked right down the middle of the sidewalk. Even when she got up to the long lines that led to the turnstiles, everyone moved aside. An older gentleman immediately slipped his quarter into the turnstile as she entered. She simply floated by.

It was unbelievable that despite all the policemen, soldiers, and federal officials, no one bothered to try and stop her. Everyone just stared.

She walked right up to the middle of the bridge, the crowd continuing to part for her, and she faced east at the railing.

"Whatsoever you do to the least of my brothers, that you do unto me," she sang.

A crowd had gathered around her, amazed, bewildered, not knowing what to do at all.

Rosa finished her song and, with one swift move, pulled herself up unto the rail, her legs over the top on the river side, her white patent-leather shoes hooked around two of the rail bars, facing east, looking for God.

Everyone gasped.

Rosa sang her heart out, perched on that metal rail like a bird.

Someone ran to get the police.

The whole incident was over in a matter of minutes. Just as two or three policemen got to the scene, an eighteen-wheeler honked loudly and screeched to a halt almost directly in front of them. Rosa turned around to look, and when she did, one of the policemen ran up to her, grabbed her, and pulled her off the rail. Then, after the policeman realized that she would not resist, he cradled her in his arms like a little child and started walking back to the American side. She plucked the petals from the flowers and, with each step the policeman took, she threw another petal over the rail into the river. "Ave, ave, ave, Maria. Ave, ave Ma-ri-i-i-a."

SOFIA stared up at an airplane in the clear blue northern Mexico sky and said, "When I was young, there were no airplanes. Imagine. No airplanes. Every time I look up into the sky and see one, I just can't believe it." Her thin cotton dress was flapping in the hot breeze, big blue flowers on it, like the sky. She stood there staring for a long time, watching the fluffy white line that the airplane left behind, curving across the sky. The sky became a ceiling, el cielo. And Sofia became the sky.

She was a child, really, just fifteen years old, when she met him first in the tiny Mexican village. She knew immediately that she loved him.

She sat next to her sister, Angela Gloria, the night she met him during a dance at the plaza. Lowering her eyes demurely when he asked her to dance meant she was interested, although she said no to him that night. She'd wait until the next dance the following week; then she would say yes. But who was he? The gossip started immediately.

The women, all sitting in a huge circle around the dance floor, began asking, *"¿Quién es ese hombre?"*

You could see the heads turn as the question was whispered around the dance floor, as if they were playing a nasty game of "pass it on" at a bridal shower. Before the night was over, she knew who he was.

⁂

Forty-seven years later, she was waiting for him to come home from work on the Mexican side in the evening, as she did every night.

⁂

On her way to the bridge, she stopped at the Woolworth's to buy an ice cream sandwich to try and cool off; the oppressive heat and humidity were weighing her down. She was tired, and it was hot, so, so hot. Since her husband had not come home last night, she knew that something was wrong.

After she bought her ice cream sandwich, she stood four blocks from the bridge, watching the commotion. She hoped with her whole heart that her husband had not gotten into any kind of trouble. He had never done this before, and she really did not know what to do; he was old, you know.

She had spent the whole night awake, waiting for him in her rocking chair, repositioning the electric fan over and over again because it was so hot and because she was so nervous. The soft-boiled eggs remained in their shells in his favorite bowl on the kitchen table. She saw the sun rise through the screen door, and she began to cry. There was no one she could call except the police, and the police could probably do nothing for her since he was on the other side. And the police on the other side, well, they would only try to get money from her; she knew that.

As soon as the sun comes up, she thought as tears rolled down her cheeks, I'll go across the river and find him myself.

But when she had tried to go across early in the morning, the bridge had been closed. Something was happening with the river water, and the crowd would only let her get as close as three blocks away.

She returned to her house to wait and see if they would let her cross a little later, but she fell asleep on the rocking chair until a moment ago, when she woke up with a shock and realized how late it was. Her husband was still not home. And she felt as if she had lost a whole year from her life.

She showered quickly, perspiring even while she showered, it was so hot. She showered quickly, without thinking, so upset was she about her missing husband. As she made her way back to the bridge, she noticed she had not rinsed off well enough, discovering shampoo dripping from her ear as she walked. She realized that she had slept right through a rainstorm: the hot pavement was wet and steaming. The hot, soapy liquid was dripping down her neck.

Now she stood there, a few blocks away from the bridge, her ice cream sandwich melting, dripping onto her hand, staring toward the bridge, focusing on nothing except for the worry inside of her, licking the ice cream from her hand.

She hesitated to go to the bridge, afraid of his not being there, afraid of not seeing him, but she nonetheless took her first step south, throwing her neapolitan-soaked napkin into a trash-filled box. She bit open a Wet-Nap that she pulled out of her coin purse, wiped her hands and her lips, and walked to the bridge. The cooling towel felt good around her mouth.

She almost turned around to go back home; she couldn't bear the thought of not finding him. But something pulled her. Something made her look toward the bridge and walk. There were so many people around her, and she was so short. She had to stand on her tiptoes to see and then barely as she searched for her husband over the people, oh so tall, waiting in line to cross the bridge.

"*Es la sangre de Dios*," said a woman in line at the turnstile to a reporter three people in front of her. Sofia was religious, but she thought it ridiculous that someone thought that the dirty water in that river was now the blood of God.

Frantic, she pushed her way past the woman and the reporter, and because she was so small, she easily wove her way through the throng. Looking desperately for her husband, she bumped into a woman, halfway down the bridge, who was completely soaked and bent over in pain.

"*¿Hija mía, qué te pasa?*" she said, asking the woman what was the matter.

Then Sofia saw her belly.

The woman was falling to the ground; Sofia did what she could to help the woman gently to the concrete. Two old men also came to her aid. The child was coming.

The woman yelled loudly, the pain was so great. The child was coming. Sofia took her plastic coin purse and placed it in the woman's mouth; the woman bit into it instinctively, and her legs spread open. The blood began to flow, the skin between her legs had torn, and her child's wet, dark, black hair was beginning to show.

The coin purse fell out of the woman's mouth, the child slipped out quickly from inside of her, and both let out a piercing yell. Sofia took the child into her skirt and wiped it tenderly. Still kneeling, she raised the child to the heavens, blood dripping from the baby onto her face, onto the sidewalk, into the red, red water of the river. The breeze from the helicopter above cooled them, the breeze that filled the bridge with the smell of mulberries and birth.

12

soledad

THE tempestuous sky that swept in from nowhere that afternoon suddenly burst open with a crack, and the thick downpour of hot South Texas rain mingled with the warm water of Soledad's womb, dripping slowly down her legs as she walked toward the American side to have her baby. Then, as suddenly as it had begun, the rain stopped. The sky turned clear, bright, hot, electric. The rain evaporated from her face; her eyes were no longer heavy.

She could see clearly now.

She would name her baby Clara.

As she stepped onto the bridge, she felt a sudden pain, like a blow. She squatted immediately, naturally, instinctively. Someone was helping her. She was so grateful. As she looked down, over her belly, between her legs, the skin tore as if it were a piece of paper, her dark pubic hair was soaked in blood, and she saw her child's head break through. She let out a loud scream and almost fainted.

The strong smell of mulberries, a sudden wind, the helicopter droning above brought her to. She was sitting in a small pool of blood. The pain was gone. She was hungry. She thought she heard an ambulance. She looked down again and saw the cord still between her legs. She followed it up to the arms of the woman kneeling in front of her who, she now remembered, had been helping her. She was holding the child in the air in front of her, obviously praying. Soledad smiled at her child, still squirming and crying. Soledad took a deep, deep breath of the air that smelled of mulberries and prayed too, softly, "Clara. Clara. Clara."

THE sister noticed the Special Report flashing on the miniature portable TV given to her by one of her students, okayed by the Mother Superior—"but only for special events" (the Pope was visiting South Texas that summer). Sister Adela watched in disbelief as Tomasita's personal photographs flashed across the screen—the picture taken when the nuns had given her an award and asked the monsignor to celebrate a special mass in her honor—pictures of her and her husband—and at last, three of the four small pictures in a strip Tomasita had taken at the booth at Woolworth's downtown for her green card.

The newscaster ended the special report with, "This woman is now being sought for questioning by the Mexican authorities in connection with events surrounding the mysterious color of the waters of the Rio Grande." Sister Adela just sat there in front of the tiny TV and cried, remembering her life in Mexico City and how it had been shattered by one Special Report after another.

She remembered the hill of the tenement in which she lived with her father, her mother, and her brother, Javier, on the outskirts of Mexico City. Special Report: "A bus has crashed into a Pemex gasoline truck as it took a sharp curve along the treacherous road between Taxco and *La Capital*." Adela collapsed.

The giant fireball of steel and rubber and flesh fell half a mile down the steep mountainside. No bodies had been recovered. There were no survivors. Her parents had been on that bus.

Her brother found her on the floor of the tiny living room when he came back from the market with a wire basket full of eggs. Adelita was covered in perspiration and crying uncontrollably.

"Adelita. Adelita, *linda*, everything will be all right. Everything happens for a reason. Don't you remember, that's what Dad always said," he told her in Spanish after they had confirmed the misfortune. And so she mustered the strength, as her mother had taught her to do, to get on a bus and travel the same treacherous road to Taxco for the funeral.

The government-owned oil-and-gas company paid for fifty-seven empty, flower-covered caskets, all carried up the steep streets of Taxco by Pemex workers to the church. They lined the entire street, from the altar to the other side of the plaza, as the bishop prayed for the souls in the empty coffins. A huge flower mural covered the entire façade of the church, ordered by Pemex, of course. Adelita and Javier, sixteen and eighteen years old, stood outside the church, holding hands, crying—there were so many people, they could not get in.

A week after the funeral, over her brother's protests, Adelita took a job as a maid in the ritzy Polanco section of the city to help put him through school and to pay for food and taxes on the apartment their parents had left them.

Oh, my God! she thought as she stared intently at Tomasita's image on the little television set flashing alternately with images of the Rio Grande, red as blood. Her past and all its pain was there before her once again.

Special Report: "A clash between university students and federal troops early this morning has left over thirty students dead and hundreds injured." Old, snowy television images flew through her head as if she had just seen them yesterday—burning banners, young Mexican boys and girls beaten by soldiers. A young girl, maybe her age, pulled in two directions by government German shepherds. Fires. Soldiers hosing down throngs of students. Water splashing, spraying everywhere. She remembered getting off her bed to fidget with the foil rabbit ears the old TV had for antennas so that she could see what was happening one particularly violent day during the summer of 1968. The summer when all eyes were focused on Mexico City for the Olympics. The summer they had released thousands and thousands of white doves at the Olympic stadium, the doves of peace. The summer her brother disappeared.

Afraid for her life, she ran to the ancient convent behind the hill, where the Virgen de Guadalupe had appeared to Juan Diego and married God.

The sisters gathered in the tiny chapel as the priest celebrated a funeral mass for her brother. Not even an empty casket this time. The newscasters reported body parts washing ashore just south of Acapulco. Adelita took her novitiate vows and was sent away from danger to study in the United States.

Tomasita was her *comadre*, a friend like a friend from her youth, from the past, who called her, "Adelita," not "Sister Adelita," just "Adelita," like her brother called her so long ago. She loved her dearly.

Special Report flashed onto the screen again. Tom Brokaw warned people to stay away from the river "until a full investigation is completed by the Department of the Interior and the Centers for Disease Control." The red, red waters of the Rio Grande sparkled in the background.

The nun heard someone fidgeting with the lock on the kitchen door. It startled her.

14

tomasita

SHE sat there, kneeling at the river's edge, washing her dishes intently, when the pot in which she had burned the beans slipped out of her hands and fell with a thud into the heavy washtub. *¡Diosito Santo!* she thought. It's broken. It's broken. She began to cry because the pot had been her grandmother's. Afraid to look at the shards of clay under the suds, she raised her dark, calloused hands up to her face. Slowly she fell to the ground like a wet kitchen towel, the sandy earth beneath her cheek like a pillow. She lay there for a long time, thinking of her grandmother and her mother, both long gone, standing, stirring beans over an open fire.

She rose up slowly, taking the shards of clay out of the bottom of the washtub, searching for them with her fingers under the other dishes as if the pieces of the broken clay pot were precious pearls. She packed them gently, one by one, into her plastic mesh bag. She finished washing her dishes and emptied her washtub into the Rio Grande, far to the west of the city, where the houses were barely houses, close to the small stream that came from the huge American factory.

She was alone. She and José had not had children. Her husband had begun to complain about a pain on either side of his face right under his ears during that cold, cold January, two years after he had started working as a waste disposal superintendent for six dollars a day for the new factory. Two purple bulbs kept growing, as if he had the plague. When he died, she had lost the small cinder-block house that the factory rented to them. Her friends had built her a two-room home by the river. She cooked a pot of beans for them the day they came to build it; a pot of beans was the only gift she had to say thanks for the wooden planks, cardboard, and green corrugated fiberglass sheets that were her home, right there by the river. The river was her backyard, her toilet, and her bath.

After she had broken the bean pot, she walked for days all along the river with her pink plastic mesh bag, collecting mulberries from the trees that grew wild along the banks. She did not seem herself; she did not feel herself. Yet she knew she had something that she had to do. She did not yet know what. She collected so many mulberries that she ended up with a mound that measured four meters across and two meters high right behind her house. She spread the mulberries over the sandy ground with a homemade bamboo rake to dry.

For months, Tomasita sat there every night by the river after she got home from ironing habits at the convent of the Salesian Sisters on the American side, grinding the dried mulberries and the pieces of clay from her broken clay pot on a large, flat sandstone until they became a powder so fine that she had to be careful that it wasn't blown away by the faint, hot, border breeze. She put the powder into the huge tin washtub, a handful at a time. Every night, when she'd finish grinding the berries and the clay, she would cover the washtub with the giant, green elephant ear leaves that grew along the banks. The night she ground the last chard of clay and the last handful of berries, she had filled the tub almost to the top. Now, bathed in perspiration, she looked up into the stars and suddenly was lost: the space inside of her was the same space she was staring into. She was nowhere and everywhere at the same time. She now knew exactly what she had to do.

At midnight, with every ounce of energy she could call forth, she dragged the huge tub of powder to the edge of the stream.

The stream that killed him, she thought as she began spreading the powder along the stream, throwing it out of a loose fist, making the sign of the cross with each toss. She spread it all the way from the big-mouthed pipe coming out of the factory wall to where the stream emptied into the river. It mixed with the mud and sludge along the stream's edge, slowly, slowly seeping into the river.

The moon was full as she threw the last handful of powder into the stream; a strange, cool gust of air coming from the river crept up her spine. She genuflected and began her walk back home and, exhausted, lay down on her bed to sleep.

If she had stayed a moment longer, she would have seen, when the moon moved out from behind the thick, white clouds that had been covering it, that the water that flowed from the stream carried the powder into the river and the waters of the Rio Grande had begun to turn a dark, dark red, like the Nile turning into blood in Cecil B. DeMille's *The Ten Commandments*, like magic.

She was awakened the following morning by an NBC news helicopter hovering over the river. She wondered what was going on, her hand shielding her tired, old eyes from the hot morning sun and the flying dust. A man hung halfway out of the helicopter, holding a huge black camera over his shoulder.

Tomasita followed the direction that the camera was pointing to and, with a gasp, saw the river, red as blood.

She stared as if she were watching a silent movie in slow motion, in total silence, for she had gone completely deaf several years before, after a bad cold, around the time of her husband's death. She also could not smell the intense scent of mulberries in the air. When she had lost her hearing, she had also lost her sense of smell.

Tomasita did not know what she had done. In less than twelve hours, the waters of the Rio Grande had turned a dark red for miles and miles, and the river was now beginning to empty its redness into the Gulf of Mexico.

When the helicopter finally flew away, in the distance she saw Mexican soldiers dressed in protective clothing poking at the stream with long, shiny steel poles that had little, stainless steel buckets attached to their ends. They carried shiny black machine guns too.

What have I done? she thought, looking at her red, stained hands. "*Diosito Santo*, they're going to find me!" she whispered to herself.

Alarmed, she ran into her house to hide.

At first, she stayed there, breathing heavily, perspiring, leaning against the false door her friends had put up, thinking, thinking, thinking, What do I do now, *Diosito Santo*? What do I do now? Then she grabbed her coin purse and her green card and began to make her way toward the bridge to the American side, to the convent, where she knew she would be safe.

The Mexican government boarded up Tomasita's house, sealed the door and windows with adhesive notices expressing the gravity of breaking in, placed a soldier on twenty-four-hour guard, and sealed off the area with orange ropes, cardboard signs warning of contamination hanging from them.

The soldiers had followed the track that she had left as she desperately pulled the heavy tub of powdered mulberries and clay to the edge of the stream next to the factory. Inside the house, behind the now dilapidated armoire her husband had bought for her many years ago as a gift for their first anniversary, the soldiers found the tub, a dark red, powdery residue staining it.

⁂

A thunderstorm was brewing as she walked the almost four miles to the city. It was nearly noon. The sky got dark, the air, hot. And from the outskirts of the city, where the sky thundered suddenly and the clouds began to pour, she walked another four miles to the bridge. She was soaked to the skin.

As she walked past the guard on the Mexican side, she felt a palpitation in her heart. She felt as if she was going to die. She knew that she would be found out.

She wasn't. She paid the toll, and as she stepped onto the bridge, she saw the commotion just beginning. Television cameras. Policemen everywhere.

No one even noticed her. People were staring and pointing down into the river. She knew what they were looking at, and she felt nervous again. She did not know how to act, what to do. She no longer knew if she was soaked in rain or perspiration.

She stared into nothing again, as she had done the night before—until the sudden, sharp, piercing cry of a baby broke the silence of many years. She could hear! Confused, stumbling, her hands now shielding her ears from the shouting officials and the honking trucks and the loud helicopters above her, she took a few steps forward, remembering her mission to get across the bridge. She saw two old men squatting in front of a woman giving birth.

She was astonished—still in a daze. As the cars and trucks passed by, as helicopters hovered above the scene, as people yelled for ambulances all around, she saw a beautiful old woman kneeling on the hot pavement in front of the woman, staring with piercing hazel eyes toward the blue sky, lifting a child over her head as if to offer it to the heavens, the umbilical cord still connected to its mother, blood slowly seeping down her hands, the child yelling its pain of birth.

She walked toward the child and placed her red, stained hand on the child's forehead and walked on, the smell of the newborn child mixed with the scent of mulberries on her hands. She did not see the red stain she left in the center of the baby's forehead as she pushed her way through the crowd to reach the American side.

⁂

The city bus dropped her off right in front of the convent. She'd been ironing for the good sisters for over fifteen years. They loved her as if she were theirs, as if she were one of the sacred family. Still nervous, she tried to put her key into the door, but she was so agitated, she fumbled and could not get it in. She was finally able to put the key in the hole. She stumbled into the convent through the back entrance right by the kitchen.

The nun sat in the kitchen, staring intently at the little television in front of her, a flood of memories streaming from her eyes.

Startled, the sister looked at Tomasita, soaked in rain and perspiration, her hair disheveled, her eyes gone mad—or so it seemed.

Tomasita approached her and embraced her; tears poured from Tomasita's eyes. The nun made her sit down at the small kitchen table and placed the kettle on the stove to boil some water for a sour orange leaf tea to calm Tomasita's nerves.

And as she turned and looked at her, Tomasita placed her hands, palms up, deep dark red, on the table.

Sister Adela had learned to read her face, to know what she needed, what she wanted—the spray bottle for the liquid starch, the plastic trash bags to sort the clothes into, the extension cord for the iron—all they had to do was look at each other, and the nun would say, "Wait just one minute, I'll get it for you."

She came over to the table and sat in front of Tomasita. Spooning a big dollop of honey into the tea, she placed the teacup into Tomasita's extended hands and gently helped Tomasita close her clammy hands around the warmth to conceal the red. Not a word was said.

The nun hid Tomasita in an empty dorm room in the back of the convent, a room the novices used before they took their first vows. It was a simple space: an iron bed, a little table, a big crucifix on the wall over the bed.

And in that room, all she did was iron. She ironed and ironed and ironed and ironed for hours throughout the afternoon into the night with shocking intensity, thinking of nothing but ironing. It seemed that she ironed, not to finish ironing, but simply to iron.

Sister Adela snuck into the room every hour or so to see how she was doing. She still had not figured out how to tell the Mother Superior.

Tomasita continued ironing, ironing, thinking of nothing, until early in the morning, before the sun came up. Something flashed through her mind that made her feel as if the top of her head was on fire. During what seemed both a split second and an eternity, she saw herself burning, the flesh falling off her bones, her hair disappearing, her nails melting, her bones shattering from an intense fire until there was nothing left. A final image was now seared into her brain, the brown, feathery remains of the love letters her husband had written to her, floating through the air. She would go back to the river in the end, and he would be with her. She smiled, in peace at the thought of him. She felt an incredible calm. She felt the universe inside of her. She realized that she was made of clay and that to the Rio Grande the clay would be returned.

Then from this peace was born an incomprehensible desire, a desire similar to the one that overtook her last night by the river. Her eyes glazed over. She began going through the pile of black habits lying on the edge of her bed, looking for one that would fit her.

The letters were hidden in the old armoire her husband had given her for their first wedding anniversary, in the secret hiding place he had created in one of the drawers inside the piece of furniture.

"So you can hide the money we save to buy a house. One day, Tomasita," her husband had said, pointing to the secret drawer, "with the money we save in there, we'll have our own little house."

The drawer was never filled; they never had any extra money; it always seemed to disappear. One afternoon a few years after her husband had built the secret hiding place, knowing they would never be able to save any money, she slipped the love letters he had written to her into the secret space.

She knew by now because Sister Adela had told her that her photos had been on TV, that the soldiers had taken the photos she and her husband had taken—the one of them standing in front of Horse Tail Falls in Monterrey during their honeymoon, the picture of the both of them standing proudly in front of the small cinder-block home the company had rented to them, he, shielding the sun from his face with his up-turned palm, a big old smile on his leathery face. Tomasita knew that the letters were still there, in her small, sweet house by the river. She would get them back, no matter what. She would hold them in her hands when that incredible fire she had felt that afternoon finally consumed her. She would return with the letters and her sorrow to the mud of the Rio Grande.

Before the nuns arose, Tomasita was walking in the dark toward the Rio Grande, toward the bridge. Several hours later, worried and unable to sleep, Sister Adela found Tomasita gone, the back door unlocked. Praying out loud, Adelita began to walk, that dark, hot morning, toward the bridge.

⁂

Tomasita found herself behind a huge cactus plant, in the dark, lying flat on the ground, holding the silver rosary the Mother Superior had given her, her cheek once again against the soft, sandy earth by the river.

Some had stared at her as she crossed the bridge because it was so early in the morning.

The officials at the bridge had simply said, "Good morning, Mother," and had waved her through, not asking her for her papers or for a list of what she was bringing from the United States since she had nothing.

An old woman on the bus, obviously poor and tired in her tattered housedress, the smell of squalor coming from her hair, asked Tomasita to pray for her.

"I have high blood sugar," said the old woman, "and my legs grow numb as soon as the sun sets in the evening."

"Pray for me," Tomasita said to the woman, "and I will pray for you."

She gave the woman a holy picture of Saint Clarisa, the saint that keeps things hidden from others. She had found the picture in the drawer of the small table by the bed at the convent, and she had brought it with her that morning after asking Saint Clarisa to help keep her hidden when she got to her old backyard.

"Say the prayer that's on the back of the picture in my name. Pray it real hard, and I promise to say a novena for you when I get back to the convent," she said to the old woman.

With a nervous smile, she waved at the woman and got off of the bus half a block from the unpaved path that led to her old house.

Filled with a sense of nostalgia, a feeling of sheer happiness running through her body like electricity, she planned her next move.

If and when that soldier moves from the door, and he will have to eat or go to pee or something, she thought under the cactus, I'll do it.

Just as she had thought, after only a few minutes of waiting, she saw the soldier walk off into the grove of mulberry trees by the river. She knew she would not have much time, so she pushed herself off the ground, wrapped the black veil around her like a shawl so that the white part of the habit around her face would not show, and walked quickly to the door of her old home.

When she got there, the only thing that she saw was the heavy, metal lock on the door.

What am I going to do now? she thought. The soldier's going to come back. What am I going to do now? I can't even see in this darkness. Oh, Mother of God, what am I going to do now?

She ran to the edge of the river and, with the help of the light of the moon, spotted a large, white limestone. She bent over to pick it up, hands trembling, and quickly made her way back to the door. Somehow she lifted the heavy stone over her head and threw it at the lock holding the door shut. The sandstone exploded. The metal lock snapped right off the door. She slipped inside and closed the door behind her. She stood with her back against the door just as she had done the morning the soldiers had come, perspiring heavily in the hot, heavy habit, panting. She pulled out the lighter she had placed up her sleeve and flicked it on. There it was, in the corner.

It was barely intact, held up by the wall. All around it, on the dirt floor, her clothes were scattered, caked with mud, covered in footprints. She saw that the drawers were missing! A heaviness took over her heart. Tears fell from her eyes. She held the lighter in her hand, her arm stretched out in front of her, and she shone the light around the small room.

There they were, both drawers, one broken up, in the corner on the other side of her old bed. Quickly she made her way across the room, catching the hem of the habit on the corner of the bed, ripping it. The sound of the fabric tearing made her freeze like a deer hearing noises in the middle of the night. Her thumb came off the lighter. The light went off. She stood there, frozen, for what seemed a long time. She could not move. She was more afraid that the letters would be missing, that they had been found, than of the soldier coming back and finding her.

Finally, in the dark, reading the furniture with her hands and the floor with her shoes like Braille, she found herself kneeling in front of the drawers. With her fingers, she felt the bottom of one of the drawers until she found the little wooden bump. When she pushed it gently, the false bottom popped up. Trembling, she reached into the compartment. The letters were there. Tomasita wept.

Suddenly she heard the door open behind her, and with a jerk, she turned around and lit the lighter. The soldier stood still. A sort of nervous energy flowed between them.

The soldier could not shoot. He didn't know if it was because she was a nun or because he knew it was her or because he saw the stars in her eyes, but he could not shoot. For a moment, they both understood what neither of them really understood. For a moment, they both knew love in its purest and simplest form.

She grabbed the letters and walked right by him saying, "*Que Dios te bendiga, hijo*," and placed her red-stained hand tenderly on his cheek. He saw a tiny spark of static electricity break the darkness when she touched him. And he awoke from his trance.

Gunfire exploded behind her. He had to act as if he had fired at her. She saw the light coming from the gun over her shoulder as she ran down the path. When she had passed the orange cords, she stopped for a moment to catch her breath and to pull the habit over her head. She rolled the black habit into a bundle and hid it under a small thornbush. She turned around when she saw the rosary on the ground and picked it up along with some sandy dirt and held it tightly in her hand.

The soldier was on the portable phone. He had strict orders not to leave his post under any circumstances, so he could not be blamed for not following Tomasita. Almost immediately, the sirens could be heard. The armed forces were on high alert.

The soldier told them she was wearing a habit, even though he knew that she would probably take it off.

She hid behind a dumpster as she reached the outskirts of the city. It was still dark. She could hear the sirens everywhere. She saw a black jeep, the Federales, speed across the intersection a few blocks away. She knew that she would die, and right there and then, behind the large, dark green dumpster, two empty cans of Green Giant sweet baby peas at her feet, she made her peace with God, still holding the dirt and the cross tightly in her hand.

She walked out from behind the dumpster majestically; she had broken through. Tomasita headed toward the bridge.

She walked several blocks normally; no one even looked. A white police car sped by right past her. Her breathing was steady and low.

At the corner, a horse and carriage pulled up in front of her. It was an old, old horse and an old, old man. The horse's hair was falling off in clumps; there were large spots where the horse had no hair at all, especially around the stomach, where the horse's ribs showed its emaciation. The old man's shirt was unbuttoned, a yellowed, white handkerchief tied around his neck; his ribs showed through as well.

But the carriage. Oh, the carriage! It was covered with hundreds of plastic flowers that to Tomasita seemed to glow under the yellow streetlamp. But then, everything seemed to glow. A wooden sign, a wide split right down the center of "Special Horse Ride—$2.00 (American)," hung from rusted wire from the wooden steps that were covered in worn-out tire strips that led onto the carriage.

The old man looked at her, tipped his hat, and said, "*¿A dónde la llevo, señora?*"

"*El puente*," she answered, and reached for the hand he offered to help her step into the carriage as if she were being led onto a dance floor.

She rode through the streets of her life, a sweet smile on her face, tears flowing from her eyes. An old, portable radio, held together by dried masking tape that the old man carried, played "Solamente una Vez."

The old man pulled on the horse's flower-covered reins right in front of the Plaza Juarez, several blocks from the bridge, as close as he could get—the commotion at its highest, a river of people flowing over a river of water.

The old man held his hand out to Tomasita again. She took it, stepped out of the carriage, and thanked him, "*Que Dios se lo pague*," placing the rosary and the dirt she had been desperately holding into his hands. He bowed his head to her and touched his hat.

The police were everywhere. She breathed steadily and walked right past them at the corner of the plaza, by the liquor store, at the entrance to the bridge. She took a deep breath, then she got lost in the crowd. She had never felt so full of life.

He thought he saw her out of the corner of his eye. The little kids, five- and six-year-olds, who sold Chiclets on the bridge, had gathered around him and were pulling on his green army pants, begging him to show them his rifle. He tried to shoo them away so that he could reach into his starched shirt pocket for the photocopy of Tomasita's picture, the one they had taken from her house, the one she had taken at the Woolworth's on the other side. His heart pounded. He was pretty sure that it was her, but he had to look at the bad, black-and-white copy the officials had made by the thousands to be perfectly sure.

"Use whatever force necessary" had been the order, and he had been trained to follow orders.

"Hey, mister," the kids said in Spanish, "show us your rifle," and continued to tug at his pants.

"Leave me in peace," he said to the kids, and tried to push them away, but the crowd was beginning to swell. Police cars were arriving from every direction. The press was descending on the bridge like hunters waiting for the giant buck. And the curious kept pushing their way closer and closer, jumping over and sneaking under police barricades set up to control the crowd. He did not know what to do. He saw her again, moving onto the bridge about twenty feet to his right. There was no way that he could possibly get to her. He lost sight of her and began to panic. The kids were still pulling at his pants, and one of them, playing, grabbed the rifle strap and hung off of it. He lost his nerve and pushed the kid off him with the butt of his rifle, accidentally hitting the little boy right in the mouth, making his lip bleed. The child started yelling. They were pressed together, the soldier, the rifle, the kids, and the crowd. Perspiration was running down his face. His hands were cold, clammy, and moist. He saw her again and immediately began to push his way toward her, her photocopied image now photocopied on his mind. But the crowd was tight and ready to explode. He took his rifle from his shoulder and pointed at the crowd in front of him to make them move aside. The crowd went crazy.

The throng quickly split open, and the soldier aimed his rifle right at Tomasita and yelled, *"¡Señora! Alto! Señora! Alto!"*

People began pushing and shoving, yelling and shouting, trying to run away, but they had nowhere to go. The soldier held the rifle as steadily as he could in the midst of the rioting crowd, his sweaty finger in place right on the trigger.

He yelled again, *"¡Señora! Alto!"*

But she didn't turn around.

He yelled once again, *"¡Señora! Alto!"*

Tomasita slowly turned around to face her destiny. Just as she turned around to face him, his sweaty, nervous finger slipped, and a shot rang out.

The gunfire exploded in a flash. Tomasita followed the slow motion of the bullet, like a comet on fire, coming toward her.

When the police and soldiers arrived to try and control the crowd from further rioting, and the siren of the coming ambulance parted the throng down the middle, and the newspaper reporters, TV cameras, and helicopters surrounded Tomasita, the young soldier knelt next to her and cried.

Frantically Sister Adelita arrived at the scene, pushed her way through the crowd until she broke through, and ran to Tomasita and held her tenderly until the soldiers grabbed the nun, pulled her hands behind her back, handcuffed her, and threw her in the back of a police car. Her rosary, which had slipped out of her sleeve, was dangling from the bottom of the car door, the crucifix bouncing off the still-hot pavement of the bridge like beer cans tied to the back of a wedding car as the car drove off.

A strange, cool breeze came up from the river and blew the bloodstained love letters like feathers off the sidewalk of the bridge, into the red, red waters of the Rio Grande.

On the front page of the morning papers, a close-up of Tomasita's face appeared resting on the blood-covered sidewalk of the International Bridge, a bullet hole in the middle of her forehead.

Sister Adelita stirred a large pot of pinto beans for the nuns. Her little television set on the kitchen counter flashed a photo of Tomasita, clean, in a simple white housedress, lying on a wooden table, a sea of white candles surrounding her, a handful of dark, red mulberries at her feet, an enormous sparkling emerald covering the bullet hole in her forehead.

Tom Brokaw said, "The emerald was donated by a wealthy Mexican housewife who volunteered to care for Tomasita's body. Her death has prompted an outpouring of grief in this typically quiet border community. Funeral plans are still pending."

He continued, "Please stay with us as NBC News continues," and a commercial for Dodge trucks popped onto the screen.

⁂

The good sister's tears fell into the pot of beans.

Fin
The End

Acknowledgments

I want to thank Susan Bergholz for helping me "save myself" with words. She is and always will be a dear, dear part of my soul. For this book and for the countless other beautiful things that she has done for me since the day we met, I am sincerely grateful.

All my love to my mother, Minerva, and to Ticky, Ricky, Rafa, Rodrigo, Anissa, Betty, Raul, Jamee, and the monkeys, Little Ricky and Reinaldo—you are everything to me.

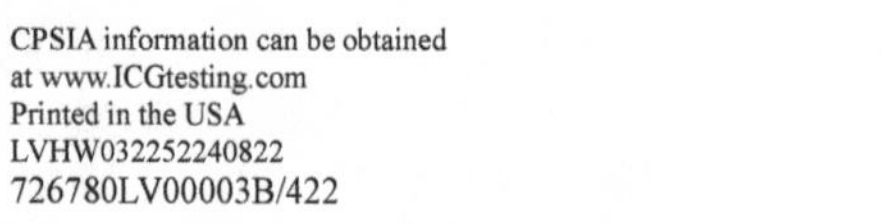
CPSIA information can be obtained
at www.ICGtesting.com
Printed in the USA
LVHW032252240822
726780LV00003B/422

9 780826 322531